Table of Contents

MW00399798

Description

Set in 1950s Italy, *Voice from the Stone* is the gothic and ghost story of Verena, a nurse, and Jakob, a young boy who has fallen silent since the sudden death of his mother Malvina. Jakob is affected by selective mutism. He has decided not to speak believing that silence can bring mummy back and considers Verena as an enemy. Verena's mission is to break Jakob's wall. Jakob fights for his isolation and communicates only with a falcon and the old stones of the ancient country house where they live. As in Henry James' masterpiece *The Turn of the Screw*, also in Raffo's haunting psychological thriller everything can be interpreted in a supernatural or non supernatural way and this ambiguity has very amazing results. The inspiration for the novel has came to the author from a real encounter with a boy who chose silence after her mother had abandoned him. Some years later, visiting a little cemetery in Switzerland, Raffo found the names Jakob and Verena written on a grave. Perfect names for his characters tormented by the mysterious voice from the stone.

Silvio Raffo

Dedication

*to all those
who in their lives
have been like
Jakob
or
Verena*

"Imperfection does not lie in truth, but in language".

ZEN MOTTO

VOICE FROM THE STONE

A NOVEL BY

Silvio Raffo

Thoughts crawl along the frozen walls of the mind as emotions once did along the soft walls of the heart.

Not all of them have the same tenacity or consistency: some are a little more than a light shiver that soon extinguishes, others penetrate with insulting violence there where the surface is less smooth, less protected from assaults; and others just give advance notice of themselves, full of possibilities, without ever taking shape.

They have crackles like dry wood burnt by fire, or pulsations like ultrasounds.

In fact, they are silent: they neither find words, nor lasting reason.

They are water snakes that attempt an impossible climb, basilisks defrauded of their ancient privilege that wear themselves out in the frustrating mirage of rehabilitation.

They don't know seasons, or climates, or tiredness; they don't prefer one particular moment to another one. Time does not concern them. Also, time is just an unpronounceable and insignificant word, a fictitious abstraction.

At the Rocciosa, maybe, time never existed. This vitreous sky, more silent than a desert, has always weighed on the

Silvio Raffo

corroded but indestructible walls by the force of a spell.

To wait for time to end in a place like this, where maybe time has never ruled, is a singular way of waiting – or, more likely, of madness. Nevertheless you wait. You continue to wait for that unique event: when thoughts stop sliding along the walls as oblique drops of rain, as blind obstinate snakes, as idle woodworms. You wait for them to give up their futile task, in order to finally give free and uncontested power to the oblivious and sighed unconsciousness of nothing.

When the misunderstanding of time will be dissolved, when past and future merge in a single eternal present, then, even to the memory of desire, any access to the City of Mind, freed in the end by the double slavery of word and thought, will be taken away.

Desire, conjecture, and words that express them can survive until something has to be or has to improve in the deceiving mechanism of time; but once its inanity has been revealed, no human impulse can disturb any more or slightly alter the infinite, omnipotent silence of the Sea of the Stone, in which conscience will be transformed.

The first vision that my memory returns to, when reconstructing the mosaic that I am about to recompose, is an indented strip of light: an odd drawing formed by the tangle of branches of powerful firs cast on the gravel stones of a path at an evening hour of last September.

I was sitting on a green bench, in the park of the Castle, right behind the old stables: my favorite corner, among those visited the least by couples and nannies, maybe because of the downward slope that slips almost suddenly into a thicket of bushes on a blind terrace, of raw stone, not particularly inviting also because of the wide cracks that ploughed it like rifts.

I was observing the game of light and shade created by the last sun, involuntarily returning back to the old childhood habit of recognizing, in those arabesques, trembling forms and imagined figures: dragons, sea horses, profiles of enchanted vessels.

Following with my eyes the plot of the inlay, almost hypnotized by the variegated and varied fringes, I saw in my field of vision an element that seemed to me immediately out of place: a piece of newspaper, that was weakly swaying

Silvio Raffo

in the shade of the fullest fir, as an insignificant wreck.

An unexplainable impulse pushed me to get up from the bench in order to pick up that piece of paper. Probably it was pure and simple curiosity, stimulated by the boredom and inactivity that weighed down the end of a day without palpitations.

It was a classifieds page of various types. It must have belonged to a women's magazine since between thick borders, with strongly highlighted headings in capital letters, there were classifieds of beauty products and domestic maintenance enriched with drawings in vivid, although faded, colors.

The page was quite crumpled, and the printed characters, faded here and there, might lead one to believe that it had been lying in the fir's shade much longer than possibly allowed by the rigid norms of order and cleanliness that ruled in the park, with its tidy flower beds and bright gravel paths where it was very seldom to see cigarette stubs and trash of any kind. Surely, it was more likely that the strong afternoon wind had naughtily diverted that tangle of messages, tying up one in the other in an incongruous order, from who knows which house or street of the city to the silent shores of the park.

Mechanically, and almost with a sense of shame, I glanced at the thick lines of the "Personal Messages", remembering the times, now remote, when, looking for a job, I devoted myself regularly to that type of reading.

Suddenly, among many banal and totally negligible requests, some words pierced my sight with the violence of an unexpected flash.

"FOR *traumatized young patient required expert person,*

available for long-term assistance and therapy."

Only the initial preposition was written in capital letters, all other words were in italic. The message ended with geographic directions absolutely insignificant to me, but I knew they corresponded to the name of a small village of the province, followed by the words "Villa La Rocciosa" and a phone number.

The emotion that had invaded me by reading that announcement froze when I saw the date stamped on the top of the page: December 10th of the previous year.

A decrepit-looking, but very distinguished man popped out from the shade of a fir: it was not the first time that I saw him, already on other days his pinched and dignified body had preceded or followed me along the paths of the park. Even on that evening he moved forward at a brisk pace for his age, leaning against a walking stick with a silver knob.

He smiled at me fatherly, something he had never done on our previous meetings, as if he realized that I was feeling uncomfortable.

I was grateful, but to not encourage him to further familiarity, I lowered my eyes and he walked beyond my bench, without sitting down by my side as I had strangely feared for a moment.

From the stables I could hear weak familiar sounds, and the humming of a tractor similar to muffled music.

What did "traumatized" mean?

And that noun, "young patient", was it implying a boy? What was his age?

In truth, I didn't understand why I was asking myself so many questions about something so distant in time, something that had probably already been solved. But I felt as if fate

Silvio Raffo

was making a fool of me. If I had seen that advertisement ten months earlier, I could have taken advantage of it and leave the Institute, from which I had been forced to go away anyway. Instead, I was given this opportunity only now, in the most fortuitous way, an offer that was surely impossible to take advantage of.

The guilty one, in any case, was me who, on the contrary of what everyone else would have done in the same situation as mine, spent their afternoons in a public park picking up pieces of old newspapers instead of buying new ones and justifying myself, at least with myself, of my unawareness.

Since three weeks ago I was free from any position of employment and I didn't feel any desire of breaking that new and almost pleasant situation of total no commitment.

I rose up from the bench feeling a slight sense of guilt. But I was also feeling another sensation, much stranger and subtler, as well as completely unmotivated: that of being observed by someone. It was as if two intense and implacable eyes were fixed on a precise point of my body, at the height of the jacket pocket, where I had automatically put the page with the advertisement. It had been such an instinctive gesture that I had not even noticed it. I realized it only at the park exit: when I saw the custodian fiddling about with the big keys of the main gate, I checked in my pocket if I had mine, since I lost them quite easily.

The old man threw me a dull look of disapproval.

"I almost locked you in the park, madam."

"Miss" I corrected him in my mind, and in the meanwhile I felt that crumbled piece of paper rustling among my fingers, as an obstinate warning.

There is someone who is trying to besiege the wall.

It must be a woman.

I can't see her face, but I feel on the other side of the surrounding walls her insistent pressure, obtuse, absolutely not meditated, actually rather fortuitous.

It is as if one of those blind insects, that maybe are called termites, dug a passage in the porous wall, already close to dissolution, unaware but favoring with stolid obstinacy the collapse that will cause its end.

In some points the wall is almost eager to collapse as I seem to perceive from a soft wheeze of the cracks: a light hiss that I trained my ear to catch through long hours of auscultation exercises.

The stone's beat has a particular way to announce itself, very different, for example, from the anxious gasping of a trapped water spring or from the deceptive glittering of the air pierced by light; not even the naïve audacity of the fire that devours, with its yellow tongues, dry twigs and powerful stumps can equal in depth and power that breath.

When I put the ear on the unstable surface of the ground, I feel the shivers of millennial roots that intertwine twisted

Silvio Raffo

in dark tangles. But there is something impure, delirious in those anxious ferments: an unexhausted swarming of putrid lymphs emitting a vulgar sound, monotonous like a buzzing.

The stone's beat has a completely different strength and elegance: it arrives only after a long, devoted listening, and it replies as a discreet echo to the heart beats. Also the more consumed and worn out is the stone, the wiser is its beat.

I feel immediately any interference or intrusion. The beat is not regular anymore, the pauses that scan it don't maintain the usual tonality of silence, the stationary suspension of sounds that they protect cracks like in a strident groan.

Musically, I think it is called innuendo, the discordant insinuation of an out of tune note in a harmonically equilibrated context.

The stone's heart continues to beat, but suffers slight changes, like lower frequencies of a radio signal.

That is what I am feeling for some hours now.

My ear is, in fact, perpetually leaning against the wall.

That dull type of termite tries to pierce it without knowing what wall it is. Probably, she thinks it is made of wood.

Should it collapse, in any case, it wouldn't be so much the wall's ruin, but rather the ruin of the insect that caused it.

No animal has or can have real power on the stone. Even in the hypothesis that the termite was able to make the wall collapse, apart from the fact that the insect itself would die, the stone would still survive.

It is also possible that it is only a temporary interference, or, as they say, transient. The insect could die before even concluding the pretentious task.

The wall has, yes, deep cracks, but most parts of its extension are very resistant.

Whatever will happen, I will only be the audience.
I will simply be watching.

Silvio Raffo

That night my sleep was disturbed by frightening visions.

I was again at the Institute where I had worked for ten years, but the rooms and the corridors were invaded by a strange smoke spiral, that was reaching up to the ceiling. In the dead of night, I was walking back and forth in the main corridor, moving with difficulty in that thick unnatural fog, without being able to distinguish the door frames, two on the right and two on the left, that led to the dormitory rooms. I knew with unequivocal certainty that the girls I was taking care of were suffocating, inactive and helpless in their beds, victims of that poisonous smoke. I myself felt penetrated and sickened by it. A heavier and heavier veil came down on my eyes forcing me to close my eyelids. Malvina's voice was calling from an indeterminable point in one of the rooms: her words were not understandable. It was only a hoarse groan that gradually was transforming in a sort of howl.

Crouched in a corner of the wall, I was listening powerless to that call.

Before I woke up, I clearly realized that it wasn't Malvina's voice anymore: now a boy was trying to spell the word *help*, taking his time obsessively on the vowel with the effect of a hiccup.

It was that sound that woke me up, but to the desperate invocation for help in the dream corresponded in real life the sound of a particularly querulous bird coming from the river banks.

It was almost sunrise, as I verified going up to the window: the fog was sailing on the water in dense and foamy volutes, very similar to the spirals of smoke in my nightmare, but, on the contrary of those, very reassuring in their soft advancing, caressing on the stagnant surface.

A strange peacefulness seemed to come up from that winking and voluptuous curtain up to my window and inside my heart. Little by little, the anguish that had been torturing me in my dream completely dissolved.

But now I was not sleepy any longer, so I stayed on lookout for maybe an hour, until the fog was gone, dispersed by the rays of sunshine and by the first boat of the morning.

It was an hour of vitreous suspension, motionless, and everything but sterile: actually, in that lucid interval of the conscience, I came to my final decision.

The possibilities of success were not many, but even if there were only one, I would have tried no matter what.

When I looked around my room, its simple and colorless furniture gave me the sensation of having bought a soul: the undone bed, the half-closed closet, the table and its only chair seemed to me a chorus of rigid but conscious witnesses. Speechless, of course: as the real witnesses of an event should always be.

Silvio Raffo

It's quite weird to notice how the so called human race, among the many possible means at his disposal to communicate, has elected the word as the privileged and optimal method.

Maybe, some form of exchange or primitive commerce or some contractual ratification regarding territories or legal sanction have taken advantage of this method, but as far as what they call human relationships, for the most decisive moments of life experience, it seems to me undeniable that the damages caused by the word are definitely more than the advantages.

I am referring to the spoken word of course, and to the feelings, or rather to those beats, longings and tensions of the soul to which men have given that name.

I don't have the slightest doubt that almost all painful experiences of a human being are due to verbal misunderstandings, to a more or less conscious violence of the word.

Sure, even silence can hurt, but at least in being silent there is the palliation of abstention, while the word has the disgusting claim of meaning. It is a real legalized lie.

Men love to deceive themselves, this is evident. The most naïve ones love to believe that it is possible to say something as if exchanging a gift to be reciprocally enriched. The fact that words, when pronounced, have no meaning seems to be of no importance.

Maybe, in most cases, it is only important that charade survives, that conversation sticks to the mechanical rules based on which the two speakers identify themselves with the performers of an act. A kind of awkward reproduction of what happens in the theater, where the script however has already been written, and therefore has at least its own independent and authentic logic, given to it by the fact that it does not have an addressee.

It is the passage from the power of thought to that of sounds that claim to mean it that destroys the essence of things.

The word addressed to any speaker is a pretentious waste.

Even these futile notes of philosophical flavor, unfounded as all philosophies, have probably a very miserable value, but they would be pure ignominy if I did translate them in a spoken speech.

I am writing them for only one reason: that they have been dictated to me by the voice from the stone.

I do not know really why that deaf panting voice has chosen me as the depository of its messages.

Maybe for the simple reason that no one else spends so much time with their ear leaning against the wall.

It isn't only the hearing, anyway, that gets pleasure from these exercises, but also the sight. Staring at a point on the wall that I cannot here reveal, I am able to see till incalculable distances, and to gradually compose scenes and situations

Silvio Raffo

that in some way concern me, with a look that is not anymore that of my physical eye, but the Eye of the Thought itself.

That woman, for example. That stolid and anomalous species of termites that I heard yesterday digging in the wall. I cannot reconstruct her face and her body, yet I can see her. She wears an old-fashioned dress, something like a nurse gown, whose color mingles with a strange fog glimmering around her person.

She is walking, in a long corridor.

I wonder what her next move will be, and in what relation this stranger is or wants to be with me.

The only word relation, that I wrote in the previous line and that I cannot therefore cancel, invites me, for its naïve absurdity, to smile.

However, I need to be very careful not to purse my lips by even a millimeter. My mouth has precise duties, and knows how to respect them.

The bus to Vigneti was leaving at twelve forty from the Market square: it was the only one of the day.

I had not thought about the return schedule until I was already seated in the bus and I was told that the only possibility to come back was at seven. I thought I was lucky: even if my visit to Villa La Rocciosa had not come to anything, as it was more than likely to be, I could anyway spend an afternoon on the hills of a village I had not visited before and almost certainly enjoy myself.

The bus left downtown faster than I had foreseen and, going around the Castle, it ran for quite a long way along the river: the poplar rows never appeared to me so melancholic. With surprise, I recognized on the opposite bank the massive and reassuring shape of my hotel and even the window of my room with the shutters half closed.

For who knows what reason, those peeled away walls, that balcony, with its miserable geraniums and the sparkling railing, seemed to me suddenly like distant forms, already part of the past, as if petrified. I felt for a moment the absurd sensation that I would never again see those places to which I had become so attached in the short period of three weeks.

Silvio Raffo

There would no longer be dreamy dawns on that balcony or the sun on the edge of the river with the first boats in the morning, ploughing the calm current.

A weird sense of nostalgia reminded me of my perfectly starched apron, hanging in the closet as a devoted servant forced too soon to rest.

Those strange thoughts disappeared together with the green water of the river that had maliciously generated them.

"Heritage of sentimentalism of childhood readings" is how the Manager Miss Ida Di Pino would have discounted them with her cold and sententious tone, shaking her big white head.

Yes, I wouldn't see her again. And sincerely I didn't think I had to feel sorry about it.

The bus had begun to wind along a steep road, full of curves: the city became smaller and smaller, and farther away, only the heavy lines of the Castle and one more time the river, now just a bright stripe, helped to distinguish the city from the adjacent villages.

The truth was that I had never had a homeland, and in any place I would stop, even for just a day, I tended to immediately and unconsciously plant roots.

For ten long years my homeland and my house had been the Institute.

Institute. This word was impressed in stone letters in the riverbed of my deepest memory: it had been with me like an indelible mark for my whole life. During my childhood, it had soothed the pain of the too disconcerting concept of orphanage; during my adolescence, it had identified with the place where, under the guide of wise teachers, I completed my cultural and professional education; during my adulthood, it had firmly fixed and circumscribed the exercise of my therapeutic functions in a well closed and ordered space.

Me and the Institute, or better the Institute and I, have always formed an indissoluble binomial.

When I had to leave it, the immediate sensation was that of a real mutilation, to which, day after day, inevitably a gradual loss of identity had been added. This second effect, to be honest, had been much less unpleasant than the first one.

Those that have never known their own roots in a certain way have never had a precise identity: now that I was suddenly without my only point of secure reference, it could have been a good moment to begin everything all over again. I didn't know who I was, I had never known it, but it wasn't ruled out that I was something that could still be fulfilled, and live even better outside the Institute than inside it.

The bus engine seemed to keep in rhythm retrospectively with memories devoted to self-destruction. I watched, almost without seeing, the ridge of the hill bristling with gorse and crushed stone, wondering where was I going to.

I was going to verify something, to confirm that I had not lost the gift of illumination. The only gift my parents had allowed me to keep.

The landscape became more and more rugged: large blocks of stone, of sharp and twisted shapes, scattered the deserted slope, giving it the aspect of a stronghold destroyed, but still inaccessible to men.

A last curve, and then on the dusty road, totally without any sign of life, appeared the sign of Vigneti. I was the

Silvio Raffo

only passenger left; while I alighted, the driver followed me with his eyes: a look of distracted curiosity, empty and insignificant, as most other people.

There are privileged points for listening, from where the voice from the stone dictates to me its messages with particular clarity and intensity.

I located them following a criterion that could be defined symmetric.

The first one I want to describe is a hollow of the surrounding wall, a few centimeters underneath the Shepherd's pedestal: the surface of the wall has here a slight recess, like a niche created on purpose for the anatomical conformation of the ear that adapts perfectly to it. It offers to the touch a sense of coldness like that of a rock and does not show any kind of ripple.

From this position, it is possible to receive even very distant messages, mostly of cosmic nature.

Another strategic point is close to the corner of the wall in the living room, on the right of the veranda. Of course, the interior wall of an ordinary house has vibrations that are very different from those of the bare stone and the rock, but you need to take into account that the framework of my house is like that of a castle. Sure, the plaster of the coating slows down the communication and often makes it difficult,

Silvio Raffo

but I had the opportunity to notice that from this part of the wall come sounds of great importance in family matters, especially those concerning the behavior and the intentions of my Guardian, the one that family ties would induce me to call aunt, or more exactly grand-aunt - a word that only thinking about it causes nausea symptoms.

There is another advantageous position in the tower: it is the sinuous, soft column of a double arched window (mullioned window), the one of the central window (there are three altogether), at the base of which a tiny griffon is carved. From here it is possible to receive (and transmit) messages that I like to call planes because they are related to the descendants of the birds: the migrations of swallows, the squabbles of sparrows, some improvisations of blackbirds, and the hunting direction of the hawk.

But without any doubt the stone that has the most intense and clear voice is my mother's gravestone, in the garden of the hydrangeas.

It is a beautiful travertine slab, a bit more than half a meter high, directly planted into the ground. Written on it is only a name, MALVINA, and a date, JUNE 6, 1960.

The strip of white and dusty road that was in front of me was leading to a wretched square that the sign of a refreshment bar, called The Red Fox, was poorly trying to brighten up. All around the lot, used as parking for cars but semi-deserted, a low broken wall looked onto the valley. On the left of the restaurant, a square-shaped building of blood-red color, the hill raised again.

The real village was a bit more higher, a bunch of houses perched on the ridge of the mountain, on the edges of a slope studded with evergreens. On the side, though, the rock sank livid and dark, with no vegetation, recalling an immense marble slab that closed the village in a narrow gorge.

The only person that I met on my way was an old countrywoman that was coming down with a huge bucket full of water on her head in a precarious equilibrium.

I asked her where "Villa La Rocciosa" was, and only after I realized I had talked to her with a tone and a pronunciation that I used at the Institute with the slower children. Nevertheless she seemed not to understand: in fact, she did not reply at all and shrugged her shoulders. I had already given up the hope of getting any information from her, saying coldly

Silvio Raffo

goodbye, when she seemed to identify the place. "The House of the Statues, you mean." She spoke with a highly dialectal inflexion, and a sort of distrust. "After the church, turn right."

I walked beyond a series of houses that succeeded one another in well-ordered progression along the hill: white, cubic, not very fanciful structures with terrace roofs almost identical the one to the other, all provided with a small staircase in front of the main entrance and a forecourt embellished, in some cases, by well cultivated flower beds. On the steps of more than one door I saw old sleepy figures of black dressed women, who did not move as I passed by, eager only to continue their rest.

I came out on the church square exactly when it struck two. Those sudden bell strokes spread in the stagnant air a gloomy echo, that seemed to reverberate from the pebbles of the church yard to the massive portals overloaded with decorations and relieves; the façade was instead of rural severity in its solid surface, interrupted only by a dark and plain rose window of tiny proportions.

Following the directions I had been given, I turned right: a grey, anonymous street that a couple of shops looked onto seemed to be leading to the more lively area of the village, but after a few steps broad stairs appeared on the side, invaded by tufts of grass, seemed to me the most favorable trail towards what I was looking for and so I followed it without delay.

Before the stairs ended, the statues were already visible: the severe profiles stood out at a distance of a few meters the one from the other, like threatening fingers against the clear undefended sky. From a distance they all seemed identical, a fan of small towers protecting the estate. As I advanced along the path where the stairs had ended - a large path open to vehicles with thick bushes at the border - I began to distinguish the feminine shapes from the masculine ones: although I saw most of them from behind, some had their lower part wider and more indented than others; of some statues on the lateral wings I could slightly catch the features of their face, hair curled in aristocratic shapes, crooked hats, lacy caps or leaning sideways.

The large open gate was inviting me to enter, even if the invitation was more mocking than warm. The shape of the house, which those incredible walls surrounded as in a grip, made me think of something in between a sumptuous farmhouse and a fortalice. Grey and heavily engraved, entirely made of stone, the long façade was interrupted with geometric regularity by a series of high and narrow windows, that looked onto balconies so close to each other to appear like a single one, as the galleries of some farmhouses. Underneath the terrace-roof, other triangular shaped windows livened up the design without sweetening it. On the side, on the right, but incorporated into the central nucleus, a tower trimmed with battlement confirmed the gloom of the surrounding wall.

It wasn't possible to locate a main door, because there were at least three all equally simple, green lacquered as the shutters of the balconies; in the middle of the façade a vault porch allowed to catch a glimpse of the courtyard, shadows of farm tools and maybe of a garage.

I stopped uncertain between the courtyard and the garden shaded by a huge magnolia. While I was wondering if it was the case to call loudly (but who? what?), I saw some colored veils moving like glittering signs under the battlements of

Silvio Raffo

the tower.

The most paradoxical thing is that, since I finally recovered, everyone thinks that I became ill of an incurable disease. Or better, that I am in need of treatments that they are not able to figure out.

I realize that it is rather ridiculous to use the word "everyone" when the people I am talking about are at most three: my aunt, Alessio and the doctor.

My condition seems to be worrying, "pathological", to the people that live around me for the simple fact that they don't understand and cannot understand its real nature: they miss the fact that it is a choice. A conscious and meditated choice: that kind of decisions that most men don't have the courage to take during their whole life.

I took that decision when I was less than twenty years old: really, rather too early.

Almost everyone lives basking in a deceitful indulgence, thinking that sanity is nothing else than a state of obtuse acquiescence or pure regress. I refused to give in to this miserable compromise. With that I don't want to say that I came to perfection – I know well that perfection is only in Death – but without doubt I came to levels of higher

Silvio Raffo

consciousness and lucidity with respect to others.

If it is true that life is meaningless, the thought is really the rein of meanings. Men don't understand this: that thought gains much more power the more it gets isolated from the gangrene of life and from the daily sense.

It isn't easy to explain. Maybe I am writing this sort of Diary of the Silence also as a form of due altruism: to try to make it understandable, to illustrate the truth that I discovered; assuming that there is someone interested in it (and someone whom I – ridiculous hypothesis – can speak to).

The secret is all in the writing. The purely abstract reality of the thought finds in writing a sort of fulfillment: its only possible form, its way to be.

How could you explain otherwise that more than once what I wrote became true?

But then is it really correct to communicate a similar truth? Should I really try to make the doctor (an absurd word if you think about its etymology) understand that, as the stone has a voice that sends messages, so the writing has the power of addressing and shaping the so called real events?

On the condition, of course, that certain terms are respected.

From the doctors' point of view, these are all symptoms of paranoia, or rather of madness.

They tried to treat me in many ways. For some time, there was here a young scholar of psychiatry, by the name of Elio Forni, who devoted himself to my case with moving dedication, putting in it far more energy than nature had given him.

I felt a sort of affection for Elio Forni, but I was able to control it; that tuft of white hair on the middle of his head made him look in a funny way like a bird that was drawn in the Science Book. His patience was greater than his perspicacity.

I am sure that I taught him a lot, even if he didn't manage to bear the stress any longer and left.

When a specialist came to see me, as to any type of operation as well, I always reacted with total indifference: a behavior that on the other hand was to me perfectly natural.

My aunt, the Guardian, never really believed in the recovery that doctors and the many specialists had hinted at in the first months: on the other hand she is, as is commonly said, a fatalist woman, and with an intimate predisposition to catastrophes.

Alessio, our "man of the house", has kept with me the same dignified reserve that distinguished his behavior when I was "healthy". He keeps calling me "young master" and serving me with deference; but, in his frowning and in the uncontrollable throbbing of the veins of his temples, I can see the symptoms of his distressed perplexity.

Even before taking my final decision, these people looked at me with a sort of diffidence (I was not a very predictable subject, as they use to say). Now they look at me with pity.

On the other hand I do not pay them much attention.

I cannot: I have many other things to concentrate on.

I think that for them my state looks like an atypical kind of lethargy. And this is in part true.

A great mystic wrote:

"My life has become a sort of sleep, and everything I see seems to me a dream. I no longer feel great joys or great grieves. And if sometimes I can still slightly feel them, it is only for such a short time that I myself am surprised and left with the sensation that it was only a dream."

But what is more difficult to understand, for anyone who is interested in the experience I am referring to, is how this sort of sleep is at the same time the most vigilant state.

In this condition of sleep – or, if you prefer, of vigil - there is only one possible danger: that someone capable of catching its particular nature comes close, with the intention of interrupting it or taking part in it.

It is in fact unthinkable that the state of grace persists if you don't stay completely and perfectly on your own.

What had appeared to me as a sparkling banner had to be nothing more than an Indian style dress: a multicolored kaftan of very thin and transparent silk.

The woman who was wearing it opened the third door on the right a few moments after seeing me from the tower: her coming down with an amazing speed gave me for a moment the absurd impression of supernatural powers.

I was in front of a figure of high importance, and to who the exotic dress seemed to add more dignity: I thought immediately about the priestess of some secret religion, and that maybe my unexpected arrival had interrupted the fulfillment of a ritual.

The expression on her large face, with many wrinkles and a light make up, was illegible and only halfway questioning.

She didn't say anything and limited herself to just looking at me intently as if a careful observation had for her much more value than the usual verbal courtesies. It was clear anyway that she was expecting from me a due introduction.

I tried to overcome the embarrassment due to my grey old-fashioned dress, whose skirt was certainly too long, the shoes squat and ungraceful as those of a nurse (but what else

Silvio Raffo

had I ever been?) and I decided as debut a quite unfortunate sentence.

"It is possible that my arrival seems odd to you..."

"It doesn't seem odd to me at all" was her reply, uttered by a calm and deep voice and accompanied by a smile that, although it seemed of superiority, it also was sincerely warm. "You don't look like one of those representatives that annoy people, nor do you look like an ordinary person. You came here for a serious reason, a precise purpose."

She sent out a light but penetrating perfume, maybe of sandal. I held out with steady hand the crumpled page, with the highlighted message.

"Maybe, actually for sure, it is too late... but I wanted to try it in any case." I uttered the last words without drawing breath: "I am a nurse specialized in these types of cases".

After reading, she stared at my face lifting up her two eyes fired up with an almost savage light; she took my arm with firm grip and invited me to come in.

The entrance was quite dark; a narrow corridor led almost immediately to a staircase of faded and broken steps, with no carpet. For sure it was the servant's entrance.

The woman walked in front of me without talking and the veils of her dress rocked in front of my eyes: going up, I noticed on the walls antiquated prints, wall lights with torn fringes and the plaster that at times made it possible to catch a glimpse of the stone built walls. "As in a prison" I thought shuddering and chased away immediately that dreadful thought.

From a bare landing we went through a tangle of narrow and poorly lit corridors, and then to what had to be the main wing of the house, a gallery of portraits and closed doors, some of which gave me the odd sensation of being only painted, like the simulated trusses on the ceiling. Suddenly we arrived in a large hall, where finally space gave an idea of opening and human breath.

The woman stopped at the corner of the wall where the archway opened and invited me to follow the direction of her forefinger; the topaz that adorned it gave out a nervous glare.

On the side of a very large glass window that looked onto the back of the house, I saw the shape of a thick brown haired boy, numb on a chair that was facing the wall. His hair was the only visible mark of his physiognomy: the lines of his face that stuck to the wall, as if the cheek had been glued to it, were furthermore removed from my sight by the left hand that was pressed on the temple. The sensation he gave me was that he wanted to break down the wall. In his right hand he held tightly an object that could have been a book or a bound notebook. Altogether it was the picture of a perfect immobility.

"That is Jakob" said the woman in an undertone, but headless of the boy hearing her. "He is my nephew. He spends hours and hours in that position."

She pronounced the words in an impersonal tone, giving the sensation of desperation with no remedy.

I was simply enchanted by the vision that exceeded any of my expectations: the only thought I was able of was that, if he had moved by just one meter, it would have been a fabulous mosaic on the glass window. This way it was a splendid fresco on the wall.

"No one has ever been able to cure him" continued the aunt-priestess. "We have tried every type of treatment."

Silvio Raffo

Moved by an impulse that no reasoning could stop, I crossed the room at a quick pace. I didn't notice the collection of Asian weapons that decorated the wall on the left or the stuffed animal heads over the fireplace. My eyes were focused only on Jakob, on that wonderful pearl locked up in its own ice shell.

I stopped at the edge of the black table that separated us.

I uttered his name as if I had known him since ever, with extreme command on myself and on the situation.

"Jakob" I said. "I am Verena."

Like a tangle of knots that suddenly unties, the cheek came off the wall, the hand left the temple and the legs stretched out. Two icy blue eyes stared at me with an expression of the most intense hate. Jakob stood up revealing a height and a physical look absolutely unsuspected: in his sky blue silk pyjamas, with harmonious step but almost running, he went out from the room without doors, opposite to the corridor we had come in from.

It was as if darkness suddenly had come down in the room. I had never seen so much beauty and so much ferocity gathered together in one single creature, and I felt almost a physical pain by being deprived from that view.

Stunned, I repeated that name that inexplicably was so familiar to me.

"Jakob!"

"It is in vain to talk to him" said the deep voice behind me. "It is has been more than a year since he stopped talking."

It is not a termite, or any other insect that I thought of yesterday.

It is something much worse.

A serpent.

You can see it from her eyes, or from her cheekbones.

Her eyes are not two curved swellings placed, as in human beings, on a plane surface; instead they go down sideways towards the temples as oblique, narrow and sparkling splits. Her cheekbones so strongly pronounced and the excavated cheeks increase the sneaky sensation of a reptile, adding a spectral note. The lips are a just drawn line; they cannot open if not to hiss.

When she uttered my name, followed by hers, I felt the clear sensation that it was a rattle snake. It was a muffled voice like the voice that comes from a mouth used to chew sand.

Sure, her name could let you even think of a viper. There, maybe this is the most reliable interpretation.

Not for nothing I heard her creeping, slimy and subtle, into the cracks of the wall.

All that I have to do now is simply to decide an action plan.

Silvio Raffo

These words disgust me but they are the only ones that the vocabulary is offering me.

Unfortunately, I am sure that that woman – the Serpent – has firmly decided to stay. She has a strong temperament, made even stronger by her obtuseness and my aunt will find in her a support. She will encourage her in any way to stay. Their craziness will merge in an unusual, frightening combination. The joined madness of two virgins of their type can give birth to a kind of highly dangerous insanity, of lethal effects.

It is not excluded that they are already defining the terms of the situation. I think I can hear them talking (to be sure I could lean my ear against the wall but the agreement is that I never stop writing in the middle of a page): they are arranging the details of the Serpent's settlement at the Rocciosa. The Serpent doesn't care about money, she will accept any salary the Guardian will offer her; besides, not having a fixed address nor a real house, she will find in the villa the perfect realization of a need that has been unsatisfied up to now.

Of course, I locked the door of my room; but there is no danger that she will come upstairs this afternoon. She perfectly knows that it is in vain to try to get me out from here, to call me or to force the door.

She will wait for the next occasion to see me again, even if she already suffers the distance that separates us: from the room, where the two mad women are defining their absurd plans, to my room there is a space of at least fifty meters, and she almost feels a physical pain, as a pang that twists her coils. When the prey is far away, the serpent that, just a few moments ahead, smelled it or even saw it, feels consumed by the longing, destroyed by its lack.

I just need to stay calm, and convince myself that, the same way I foresaw her arrival, so I will be able to cause her departure.

It was a mistake to look at her the way I did before leaving the hall: hate is still a feeling, and of course she noticed it in my eyes.

I don't have to make any other mistake.

Especially I don't have to doubt that it is me, no matter how things go, who dictates the rules of the game.

I have two powers she is not aware of.

I listen to the stone and get its messages. And what I write, if I don't stop in the middle of the page and don't utter human words, can easily become true.

Silvio Raffo

"Is there the mother?" I asked her as soon as I recovered from the dismay; and the question, that had risen spontaneously, caused painful echoes, first of all inside me, as soon as I pronounced it.

She looked at me with a grave expression.

"Not any more", she replied, and lowered her eyes. "My niece died a year ago in an accident. It was a terrible misfortune that the boy unfortunately witnessed." A shadow passed through her voice. "I do not know if it is the case to talk about all the details now...."

"Madam, I am sorry" I interrupted her, while a power superior than any resistance was dictating to me the words "do you still want someone to take care of Jakob?"

She looked at me with her big dark eyes. She didn't look like a wise priestess anymore, but only a tired and descanted woman.

"I don't have much hope that this situation can be solved, but for different reasons I need someone to assist him."

"Do you think this person could be me?"

Her look regained intensity.

"I think so. Actually I am sure."

"In this case, I need to know everything there is to know about the boy. At least, when did he start showing the first symptoms of his discomfort?"

The aunt stood up and, turning her back on me, she went to the glass window: her body had regained an almost majestic authority. I noticed only then that the long grey hair was twisted with great skill in a double braid held by a black hatpin.

"Jakob has never had a normal life."

"And what is a normal life?" I asked, even if the question seemed to me quite a trite remark.

"What a normal life is has never been completely clear to me: I know that neither I nor his mother nor Jakob have had it." She hesitated, as if against her will she had to remember someone else.

I tried to make it easier for her.

"Not even ... his father?"

"Jakob never had a father."

Instinctively I was about to say: "Neither did I", but I stopped myself and waited for her to continue.

"My niece, the daughter of my only brother, should have never married. She was unfit for conjugal life. You see, she was an artist. Her life was the piano, music. She met that man during one of her *tours* ... she was a famous concert performer at not even twenty five. An Austrian sculptor, of some talent... it is he who did those horrible statues that surround the house. My niece thought that she was in love with him, and married him. Maybe she had always missed a paternal figure and was looking for protection; what I know for sure is that she wanted a son. Although she loved her career so much, she desired to be mother more than

Silvio Raffo

anything else in the world. It was as if she had foreseen her disgrace, a serious illness at the lungs that prevented her from continuing to play."

"How long did the marriage last?"

"A year, maybe a year and a month. A bit after the wedding, I went to visit my brother in India, where he had been appointed ambassador; I must confess that I left this house with pleasure, since the atmosphere here had become unbreathable. That man … he had habits too different from ours. As much as she was fragile and discreet, he was rude and vulgar. The only things he was really interested in were money and adventures with women. A pregnant wife was for him an unbearable burden and so the idea of becoming a father. When the child was born, he left without any justification. I came back from India to assist my niece during the delivery. He disappeared on the same day Jakob was born. We never had any news from him. Luckily. Except from some sporadic returns to India, I have always been here." She said this last sentence with a resigned accent. "When Jakob was two years old my niece became ill, she had to leave her activity as concert performer and lived with him and for him. Here at the Rocciosa, far away from everything and everyone."

"Didn't the boy attend some schools?"

"Yes of course, but everything that happened outside those surrounding walls and these rooms has never had any influence on him. He grew up lonely and silent, more and more morbidly attached to his mother, to his Dove, as he called her… and to these desert places. It is not normal that a child spends his childhood at the nipple of a sick mother and that his greatest form of evasion is just to wander about the woods behind a villa surrounded by statues."

"No" I agreed seriously, and a brief silence fell among us, that I interrupted again with another question. "Have you ever thought about knocking them down?"

"His mother didn't want to. She was incapable of resentment, she didn't mind them and she said that in the end those statues were the only heritage left to Jakob by his father. Maybe one day Jakob would have reproached her with their destruction, had he known about it." She took a deep breath, which maybe implied her disapproval, and at this point from the same room, from which Jakob had escaped, appeared a tall and bald man, with distinguished and sharp features, who gave me a deferential but cold look.

"Alessio is our houseman" said the woman whose name I did not yet know. "He has been with us since ever."

"Miss Pamela, I thought maybe you would like something...".

"Of course, Alessio, I think two cups of tea would be perfect." Neither she nor he waited for my approval; it was clearly understood that a guest of my type could not wish to have anything else. The man disappeared silently the same way he had come in.

"Now only the last chapter is missing" continued Pamela.

"Maybe the most important one" I completed for her.

"Since you can imagine them on your own, I am going to leave out Jakob's school successes and his passion for everything that concerns art and beauty. He had, as I told you, the habit of going for long walks in the woods around here. Seldom, when she felt well, his mother agreed to his desire for her to go with him. It was during one of these walks that the accident happened." The commotion was severely controlled. "My niece fell down from an escarpment. At the

Silvio Raffo

old funicular railway. She could have been saved, if two massive rocks had not fallen down on her. They found Jakob clinging to those stones: he had gone down the escarpment and had tried in vain to take her away from death. The combined strength of two men was needed to take him away from there. The same scene, even more excruciating, was repeated when they buried her. He wanted to be put in the grave with her." She stared again at a dead point, towards the glass of the veranda. "I obtained the permission to have some of her ashes buried in our garden; I thought that might decrease the pain of their separation. It turned out to not be a good idea: Jakob stayed seated for hours and hours with his face leaning against the gravestone, he dug with his own hands, trying in every possible way to reopen the box that contained his mother's remains. When we managed to get him back inside the house, his body was shaking with sobs as if it were on the point of smashing to pieces. Our doctor gave him a strong dose of tranquillizer and Jakob slept for a long time, all night long and good part of the following day. When he woke up, he seemed oddly calm, but since then we have never heard him saying one more word. Whatever he wants to communicate to me, he writes it on the blue sheets of his writing paper. Books, records or musical scores that I and Alessio took care to provide him with."

She placed her eyes back on me: they were grave and still, but something, like a sigh that crossed them for just a moment, revealed the great effort that had cost her to tell me all those details.

From my side I felt deeply calm, eager only to begin what for me wasn't simply a new job.

"Miss Pamela" I asked with a tone of voice maybe a bit too

loud "could I see the grave?"

We went there a bit later, coming down from stairs that were not the same as those we had used to go upstairs: wider and more massive, with smooth steps, they started from a hexagonal landing lit by a mosaic inlay that made it look like a chapel.

We passed through the studio, whose walls were covered with books and old portraits, and went out from a French window on the courtyard, at the light of a sun so strong to be almost insolent.

The garden of hydrangeas was a shaded corner of undergrowth, with a soft floor of leaves, with hedges of yews running alongside. Here as well the surrounding walls hung over with their abstruse shapes, of a severe silence (a fisherman, a high court dignitary, a lady with a Chinese fan, a robust shepherd), without disturbing the sweet and quiet peace of that dreamy shelter.

The grave was a modest rectangle of grass in the shadiest part of the garden, beyond of a small well with wall teeming with ivy.

When I read the name engraved on the gravestone, I felt a crack tearing me with terrifying violence at the height of my heart.

Silvio Raffo

I can see them from the triangle of my window.

I can follow their moves while I write (I have in fact learnt to write even without constantly looking at the piece of paper).

The Guardian has taken the Serpent to my mother. They are standing in front of the gravestone, and I just felt a slight staggering in the woman that says her name is Verena. She had a moment – a single moment, but an intense one – of momentary lapse. Her squamous carapace was pervaded by a shiver, actually more, by a shudder that almost tore her.

What could it possibly be?

I am realizing that I made another mistake: that of overestimating the power of the Serpent. Or better, to have given her too much importance since the first moment I saw her, and even before, since I began to feel her arrival. I allowed her to be for me a worry, a negative thought: *it was even me that suggested to her to settle here, to choose the Villa of Statues as her den.*

When she said my name followed by hers, I should have ignored her, and turned towards her the opaque look of indifference, not the livid one of hate.

How could I be so naïve to write in this notebook (now

what has been written cannot be anyhow erased) that that woman has a strong temperament and that she firmly intends to stay?

What I need to achieve is exactly the opposite: the only way, or at least the safest one, to neutralize her power is that of removing, even through the writing, her desire to stay.

If it were already too late, then the only alternative would simply be her destruction.

I have never really destroyed any person. Most likely I am not capable of that.

But I can destroy a serpent.

Saint George was able to do so with a dragon.

With a serpent – it is testified in the Science Book – it can be sufficient to stare at it and to repeat its same moves without looking away. You obtain this way the effect of hypnotizing your prey; after that, a sharp and rapid blow will be enough to crush definitely its head.

Silvio Raffo

It was certainly not a common name and the coincidence couldn't leave me indifferent.

Also because I had never really believed in the so called coincidences.

I managed anyway to control my emotion and I told Pamela, who almost never missed a thing, that I just had a light dizziness.

She seemed to be interested more than would have been natural, and she asked me if I had ever practiced autogenous training therapies for these disorders.

We sat down on the bench against the wall, between the little well and the grave. I replied that I suffered of dizziness only rarely and in a negligible way, but she wanted to talk just the same about some forms of psychological concentration that she had learnt in India and that she continued to practice.

Although I was not deeply interested in the subject, I pretended I was listening to her. As she was talking, I felt that a tie of affection, more and more intense, was binding me to that odd woman, so difficult to describe, here and at the same time far away, strong with a power that quite likely she had self-imposed on herself; beautiful (I realized it only now that I was observing her regular and clearly cut features), a beauty that was only to be watched. However, inside, my thoughts were still turned towards the name written on the gravestone, and the seven letters it consisted of, and that had meant a lot to me, bounced off my heart like a painful and implacable echo.

Together with that persistent anxiety, I had the sensation of being observed by careful and fierce eyes: the same sensation I had felt the evening before in the Park of the Castle, but now more insidious, almost filled with threat.

It was him of course, Jakob. Who else could it be?

Raising my eyes beyond the magnolia branches, behind one of the triangular windows, I saw a shadow moving back and I recognized the shining wave of his hair.

"You had better stay, don't you think?" Pamela was saying.

I pretended to hesitate a moment.

"I should notify the hotel, pick up my bags..."

"Alessio will take care of it tomorrow or even tonight. He needs to go to the city for some errands. If you agree, he can stop by your hotel."

"That's fine."

In spite of the anxiety that still pervaded me, I could not help being pleased with myself: in a little more than an hour, I had found not only a safe job (and already the laziness of the previous days seemed shameful to me), but maybe even the only way to give a sense back to my life.

We slowly crossed the garden and went back into the house through the room next to the library, where old couches and dark mahogany furniture were dozing reflected in opaque mirrors. Pamela took me to what she said was *my* room. On the first floor, on the opposite end to Jakob's room, the room

Silvio Raffo

was looking onto both the garden and the back of the villa. It was all tapestried with pink cretonne, it had a tall four-poster bed, an empire chest of drawers and a dressing table provided with a mirror that took up half a wall.

"It would be unwise to give you his mother's room" said Pamela after moving aside the curtains.

"I am sure this one will be perfect" I agreed and at the same time I saw a dark shadow crossing like an arrow the sky beyond the glass windows.

"It is Jakob's falcon" explained Pamela in a natural tone. "He has almost tamed it."

"So ... he speaks with it?" I was very struck by what only superficially could seem like another, trivial coincidence: the art of falconry, in fact, had been a subject of passionate studies during my adolescence.

"He expresses himself through particular guttural sounds or through gestures."

"Of course. The important thing for him is not to betray himself with meaningful words in the human language."

"You already treated a case like this, right?"

"Yes, a twelve years old girl."

Again the arrow crossed the crystal clear sky with a dart accompanied this time by an acute, stridulous sound similar to a scornful laugh.

Pamela was staring at me with a gleam of involuntary hope in her grey eyes.

"Did she recover?"

"Yes" I replied without lowering my eyes. "She recovered."

Alessio has removed the sedan from its hibernation. The station-wagon wouldn't be sufficient; it doesn't have enough authority for the solemnity of the occasion. Going down to the village is normal routine for which driving the more modest car is suitable; driving to the city instead is an extraordinary event that also requires different vehicles.

I heard everything from the stairs.

He will go to the River Hotel to pick up the Serpent's luggage. (I wonder if that woman is so diabolical that she was already sure to be gone forever when she was leaving her lodging.)

No, it is not necessary that Miss goes with Alessio, unless she really wants to. She can give him all the details.

She gave them to him: the personal objects are in a beauty case in the bathroom, all the clothes in the closet. (So she had already planned to move or did she have the habit, in fact congenital to vipers, to live every day as if it was the last one?)

She was profuse in detailed pieces of pieces of advice, with an almost pathetic tone, about an apron: a dark grey apron, on a white hanger. (It must be the one she uses for great

Silvio Raffo

occasions: a jailer vocation, like the religious one, requires first of all a specific piece of clothing.)

Her settlement at the Rocciosa was therefore faster than possibly predictable. So, this afternoon has been richer in news than an entire year.

It's really true that even for people that are extremely vigil as I am, specific deviations in the course of the events can happen. These deviations are totally unexpected. There is a limit I mean of imponderability in the inlay of developments preordained, consciously or not, by the mind. The Greeks called this limit "aprosdoketon" that can be translated approximately with the substantivized adjective "unforeseeable".

The relation between thought and will like the one between mental construction and contingent event, is rather complicated. If I concentrate at the best of my possibilities – listening or writing – I can predetermine the course of the events (on this I cannot and do not want to have doubts), but the actual problem, the real problem, is another one: when, concentrated at the most, I can feel the symptoms of a situation that is hostile to my will, or conscious desire. In short when I notice that something absolutely unwanted is about to happen, or has already happened, this happens for a weakness of the will that caused a temporary distraction of the mind – or do we need to admit that the omnipotence of the binomial mind-will has its limits (and every aprosdoketon would be the clearest proof of those limits) and that in short even if you are always watchful, some piece of the mosaic can be placed on its own and distort the whole picture?

I am wondering in what way that woman got in contact with me? What senseless conjunctions of elements allowed that? Was it the effect of a derailment of my course (as if I were the train driver that at times can turn into the wrong track) or was it something completely inevitable (that is other hidden drivers, and stronger than me, are able to get me out of my route and they do so just for hostility towards me)?

This hypothesis – that I am forced to take into account although it is unbearable to me - would imply that I am not the only one that can guide the course of the events.

But there is another hypothesis, maybe even more chilling: that even if I am the only driver of the events that concern me, I could even want things that can harm me.

If yesterday, for the first time, I had not felt the viper creeping into the wall, she would not have been able to come so far. Wasn't it maybe myself to write, on this notebook, that "in some points the wall is almost anxious to collapse?". How could I write something like that?

The answer is simple and terrifying: the voice from the stone, as always, dictated me the message and I transcribed it.

The Guardian is knocking at the door. I cannot stop in the middle of the page, so, of course, I will not open.

She is smart enough to understand it. She speaks from behind the door loudly enough so that I can hear her. She says: "Miss Verena will stay here for some time. Do you agree, Jakob?".

(Verena: the name of a German saint, patron of Basel, given to a serpent who knows by whom.)

Without stopping writing, I beat very quickly the palm of the hand on the desk shelf: she knows that this means "Yes" or, indifferently, "It doesn't regard me".

Silvio Raffo

So I want it to be. So it will be.

I will go down for dinner at the usual time, dressed as is suitable, keeping an absolute natural behavior.

Actually, if I will feel like doing so, I will go down even before dinner and I don't exclude the possibility of taking a short walk with Nigro.

It was strange that I had not felt the desire of going back to the hotel, at least to personally pick up my luggage and to say goodbye to the balcony on the river and to the geraniums.

Or maybe it was natural. Didn't I have the sensation a few hours earlier on the bus that I was going away from those places without the prospect of coming back?

Certain premonitions, certain coincidences are never fortuitous. Too many times I had already verified that.

Although it is better to avoid talking about these things with other people.

The director Miss Ida Di Pino, in whom I had once had the weakness of confiding in, had been quite scornful.

"D'Angelo" she said putting on the thick frame glasses of ochre color "you never have to forget to be a scientific operator. This is your qualification. You have excellent abilities as a speech therapist and you are particularly capable of dealing with a certain type of retarded or traumatized subjects. Why don't you forget about these day-dreams? They can only harm your professionalism and I don't want to hear about this anymore."

As if I had presented her who knows what type of ridiculous

Silvio Raffo

phenomena or had claimed to be a clairvoyant.

She thought I suffered from a sort of paranoid mania: "the sorceress complex". In these terms she really expressed herself when she had to write a report about my responsibility in the case of Malvina and I had found myself completely powerless.

But it had been a lesson for me. I would never talk again with anyone about things that happened to me: they would just be private episodes and I wouldn't give them so much importance anymore.

From my triangular window I was looking at the powerful shape of the magnolia, the well covered with ivy, and the bare gravestone.

The pale and sickly face of Ida Di Pino was nothing more than a memory now, a pale shade of the past.

I was perfectly sure that life was that day at a decisive crossroads. And the direction would have been the one that I would be choosing.

Pamela took me to visit the back of the villa: a third of the semicircle was occupied by a small nymphaeum, shaped like a T, and with an incredibly blue water, surmounted by four little stone elephants with their trunks raised high; a dense pergola and a garage (that once had been the stable) bordered the surrounding walls in the middle of which a rusty gate between two statues of sileni particularly deformed, was leading to the most neglected part of the estate: through a path on which the thick grass and the briars made it at times difficult to walk, we arrived up to a crag, where at least a dozen of white houses of the same dimension were lined up in a beautiful order.

"The beehives" Pamela said, showing them to me. "Alessio

is in charge of them, among the many other things, he is also a very expert beekeeper."

She had changed clothes and seemed a different person: a toned down tartan skirt and a beige cardigan had taken the place of the Indian veils; I was in front of a perfect example of British elegance.

"From this side the estate trespasses into the woods." Following the direction of her finger I saw beyond the beehives a thick scrub of larches and birches, where the path seemed to stop, and farther down rows of vines that finally justified the name of the village. The declining slope, punctuated by brooms and stones, seemed to disappear in an abyss. Opposite, the flat and dark slab of the mountain, overhanging on the greenery, threatened, more than protecting it, the innocent vegetation. But a whitish and shapeless structure, that from my prospective gave the impression of an odd outgrowth of the slope, was what caught my attention at the most.

As if she had read my thought, Pamela completed it.

" It is the old funicular railway." She looked away, lowering the tone of her voice. "Where the accident happened."

I didn't say anything. On the way back we met Jakob. He was wearing a brown fustian suit that gave him an inadequate hunter look: we was going up along the path a few steps from the gate and didn't change his expression at all when he saw us. He seemed to be engrossed in an operation from which no one would be able to distract him: even before seeing the glove on his right hand, I realized it was the falcon.

The bird in fact appeared a bit after him as if it were following him and rested on the highest branch of a larch.

The trail was quite narrow and Jakob moved aside stiffening

Silvio Raffo

his entire body as if terrified of being grazed; the smile he gave me was absolutely vacuous, too impersonal anyway for not being calculated.

I smiled at him without stopping.

"Hi Jakob. Enjoy your walk."

Even the falcon looked at me with a definitely hostile eye. The bluish shade of the beak, in harmony with the grey streaks of the feathers, gave it a noble look, softening the ferocity congenital to its breed.

At the gate I turned around: both had moved, but the falcon had overtaken Jakob although its flight was still at a low altitude.

At dinner it was a competition of high level and strategic tactics. Jakob was sitting at the head of the table, as his aunt; I was sitting in between and in front of the glass window. Alessio, who had come back home since a bit more than half an hour, was serving us the dishes on silver trays.

Jakob was controlling himself impeccably: he was quite confident with his signs. A slight move with his lifted hand indicated that he didn't want any more food, with signs equally eloquent he asked for dressings, and more than once he even turned towards me with a quite detached and imperious note.

I was talking about harmless subjects with Pamela and reserved for him quick fortuitous observations ("I see that you don't like roast beef Jakob." "You too like quite salty dishes.") to which he replied looking at me with neutral, even polite, attention, without ever compromising himself and naturally lowering his eyes as to check the food that from the plate he was bringing towards his mouth. The actions and the moves of a perfect gentleman who, I thought with an involuntarily malicious wit, was only missing the word.

"No sign of autism in the classical sense" was the metallic voice of Director Di Pino echoing in my ear. "Do you agree, D'Angelo? No basic organic dysfunction. The aphasia has to do with a schizoid syndrome. '*Elective Muteness*' as our manual would define it. And anyway a definitely atypical subject, one of those that seem to be made on purpose for you".

When, mentioning the falcon, I reminded him of the tale by Federigo degli Alberighi, of the fifth day of the *Decameron*, quoting deliberately two episodes in a wrong way, his eyes even had a flash of amusement.

He withdrew nodding and moving as if dancing. While leaving the room lit up by the pale light of the candlesticks, he had in fact the step of the leading ballet-dancer who exits the scene at the end of his exhibition.

With the movements of a grave and silent ghost, who has only the noble function of serving, Alessio came in again to clean up the table from the last dishes.

The coffee ritual was taking place in the library, as I had imagined, and with a bit of embarrassment I was able to refuse it - I had never been able to drink coffee or any alcohol – accepting willingly instead a tisane. Pamela and I were sitting in the couch like two good friends, talking about knitting and gardening, and looking around I noticed that I had already established an affective relationship with those strong furniture of old fine wood, with those severe paintings and those books perfectly aligned behind the opaque windows.

Later on, I savored with almost incredulous surprise the same sensation of harmonious familiarity in the room that

Silvio Raffo

I still found hard to believe to be mine. In the corridor I had been accompanied by the notes of a piano without though daring to verify where they came from; that echo seemed to articulate my moves while I was putting in order my few things in the old walnut closet and faded down the moment I sat down at the dressing table. Although I had turned on the main light, the figure reflected in the mirror seemed to emerge from a dark shadow bottom, empty and stagnant as my past. Staring at that cold glass well, I put the hands on my gaunt face, and on the hair pulled back and almost invisible; and the small woman that was doing those moves in front of my eyes seemed to me a perfect stranger. On the contrary the unknown objects that studded the dressing table shelf, gave me the warm and reassuring sensation of an old intimacy.

From my window a good part of the surrounding wall was visible: for some minutes I stayed with my face pressed against the glass, without being able to look away from one of the statues, the highest and the most massive one, lit up askance by the moonlight. Something very weird happened then: the shepherd's head suddenly seemed to move from the bust or to split in two as if by magic. A furtive flash came from his new eyes, but it was the flash of a second – or maybe just one of those phenomena that they call optic effects because, in the time of an eyelid beat, everything was again as it was before.

Quite upset I went back to the dressing table; almost to make sure of the efficiency of my eyes, I started again to stare at my reflected image.

The stranger in the mirror took off her clothes with slow solemn gestures.

Even from the high and soft bed, welcoming like an alcove, a few minutes before midnight, I could distinguish her rigid composed figure, stretched out with joined legs as in a coffin.

The hours of the night for who knows how to live them have a revelation power that the day doesn't know. The senses are as if purified, the sight and the hearing more capable to understand those shades in which the simple but incomprehensible essence of the thought lies. The sense of smell as well intensifies and the perfumes have themselves something to reveal.

I cannot count the nights that I spent looking at the sky and the garden since the Era of Silence began.

Of course there are different posts: from the two windows in my room, from the veranda in the living room, from the double arched (mullioned) window in the tower.

During full moon nights the best post is without doubt that of the tower, from where you can contemplate both the declining ridge of the hill, with its white stones scattered in bunches, and the rare lights of the village that sparkle as small lighthouses in the dark. The statues' shapes that surround the Rocciosa in their spectral embrace send odd reflections and it can happen that the Venetian lady's fan, when observed for a long time without looking away, gets transformed into a dagger, as it was probably in the original intention of the Sculptor.

Some nights it feels as if his presence flutters in the garden; the Sculptor sidles along the surrounding wall to pay homage to each of his creatures. They are shy visits, of extreme secrecy and are returned with absolute indifference.

Of him on the other hand I don't know anything: neither where he is, assuming he is still alive, nor what his face expression is; I only hear this vague but non-existent, non-corresponded love.

During rainy nights or even better stormy nights, the view you can enjoy from the tower is the most picturesque that you can ever imagine: the magnolia branches bend under the wind's whip until they touch the ground, and the flashes light up on the statues' faces mocking laughs that the day light camouflages in the corroded shapes almost split by time.

Since only the night gives back truth to things, I trained my body to stay awake. I am sure that with the required exercise I will be able in a few months to do almost completely without sleep. Isn't it ridiculous that every night when everything gains back its real and only meaning by suspending nonsense, trades and relations to which they are forced to, human beings choose to sink into the most sterile oblivion for even a high number of hours that they could spend positively by observing and listening?

Without doubt the thought is active even during sleep, and I can testify it with my experience because, in the very few hours that I spend sleeping, it often happens that I write without any break, one page after the other, a book that is not this one to which I devote myself when I am awake: it is therefore true that the brain, or what men like to call

Silvio Raffo

with that name, carries out its functions independently from the control of will, but it is likewise true that the lucidity of conscience is the supreme value to protect together with the continuity of the observation.

From the tower in some way I rule the reign of the night together with the sleepless birds whose calls I recognize without any chance for mistakes.

During daytime this is the reign of my aunt, the Guardian. It is a sort of studio where she paints, reads and especially devotes herself to the meditation exercises that she learnt in India.

I don't deny that my aunt has a strong intelligence and even talent. I look at her paintings with some interest: they portray women, always and only women: women with veiled faces, women upset and numb in odd fetal positions, women that are undergoing a metamorphosis into butterflies or panthers. The colors are very strong, of a violence that in some paintings seems to be unjustifiable and therefore bothers me.

She knows that many nights I come up here. A narrow corridor and a wooden stair link my room directly to the tower. She also knows that I come here with my notebook to write. She doesn't say anything, as is in her habit (she actually never denied me anything): it has happened some times that we were here together, she painting and I writing, for entire hours. But generally we try to be in the tower at different times.

At this hour, in any case, for sure she sleeps in the room next to my mother's. She has a very heavy sleep: when the Dove cried, during some nights, it was always me to run to her and the Guardian continued to sleep peacefully, *contradicting her own role.*

Even the Serpent should be absorbed in a deep sleep: or maybe she is savoring, in an extended half-asleep state, the pleasure of such a soft bed in such a peculiar residence.

I decided that I won't worry about her; if I spoke of her, I did so simply for a sense of precision.

Yesterday evening, on the trail, I met her while I was going out for a short walk with Nigro, but I didn't show the least worry. Even at dinner I was composed and impeccable for the whole time.

Shortly before midnight I spied on her in her room. After playing for more than an hour, I went down in the garden and put myself behind the statue of the Good Shepherd: there is a small niche behind his back. It is a great point to look into the last rooms of the first floor. Even if for a moment I felt that our eyes had met.

I saw her leaning her face - that horrible face with those high cheekbones - against the lit up glass. And I also saw her undressing. The shadow on the wall gave the impression of a weird reluctance; the gestures were as slowed down by a vague imminent fear. With a shiver of disgust I imagined her nudity: the white skin of a wan whiteness, typical of a nun or of a sick creature that doesn't stand the sunlight, and the edges of the bones on which that rigid and wrinkled skin stretched out.

The skin of a serpent that sheds to regenerate during the night: that was maybe the scene I was witnessing. A monstrous metamorphosis, an obscene ceremony of which I had been deliberately elected to be the audience.

Luckily the show had not been very long: at the twelfth tolling of the bell the light was turned off.

I will not take into any account this episode. The presence of the Serpent at the Rocciosa cannot and doesn't have to upset me in any way.

I will attack only in case of provocation. It is also possible that there won't be any provocation. Actually, my wish is that there won't be anything between me and the Serpent.

I simply need to neutralize her, and not allow her to enter in contact with me. And she will leave.

I wrote it. And I write it again.

She will leave.

My first night at the Rocciosa was without dreams – or at least I don't remember any.

I fell asleep with some difficulty because of the inevitable thoughts that were troubling my mind, but I woke up very rested and at a late hour.

At the end of breakfast, which Alessio had served on the veranda, I asked Jakob, staring at him with extreme naturalness, if he wanted to take me to visit the wings of the house I had not seen yet.

The look he gave me had the power of confusing me: the blue of his eyes was so clear that it suggested the image of a sea in which it would have been sweet to disappear. Some lines that I had read who knows when and where came into my mind; they said that, whenever you were suddenly in front of the Mermaids, their silence was more terrible than their songs.

It was not a look of hate, as the first one I had gotten from him, and not even an absent look or one of studied indifference, as the one from the previous evening: it was the look itself of Medusa, the look of the Gorgon that petrified anyone who dared to put his eyes on her for the

Silvio Raffo

simple fact that that wasn't allowed. I had dared and now Jakob was punishing me. Then, unexpectedly, when I had still not recovered from the dismay, he rose up and, with a light bending of the head, he urged me to follow him.

Pamela, who had been assisting to the scene not without participation and almost pleased, gave me a silent sign of encouragement.

Jakob walked in front of me along the long corridor with his light pace, as an Asian dancer. I had the sensation that he was dragging me in a vortex, that from one moment to the other he would move aside and I would fall off an abyss at the sudden splitting of the floor.

Instead, he escorted me in the music room: one of the doors that seemed painted led to a room whose only furnishings was a grand piano lacquered white, with two black stools and a blue armchair with faded fringes. On the piano were scattered some musical scores, quite old to all appearances, of which I was able to read some titles: *Child scenes, The first caress, Nocturne.* On the walls a series of tidily aligned pictures portrayed a slim and blonde woman, very similar to Jakob, intent on playing, receiving cups, and bowing from a stage in front of an audience.

Jakob stayed on the threshold, in a rigid and poised pose that looked like that of a hotel usher who was showing the room to a client.

"I am rather ignorant about music" I said avoiding looking at him. "My tastes are guided only by feelings. Schumann is anyway a composer that I love. I hope that sooner or later you will let me hear some of his music."

It was in some way a question: I was asking him if he

played the piano.

He nodded, always without showing the least involvement, with a neutral look, and I understood that he considered concluded the visit to the music room.

The next door gave access to a sort of studio, where I noticed an imposing walnut writing-desk, cluttered up with all kind of things: old paperweights, inkpots, candelabras, stamps, epoch portraits. They looked like antiques in special offer at a charity fair; the wallpaper, ripped in more than one place, depicted arcadic scenes in clear contrast with the severity of the black chest of drawers and the small bookcase of rough and squared lines.

Almost at the end of the corridor (as I was foreseeing Jakob didn't let me visit his mother's room nor his own), a red curtain, moved aside decisively, revealed a wrought iron spiral staircase that connected the first to the second floor: nothing more than a labyrinthine tangle of lofts, a part of which was a wide skylight packed with old furniture.

Jakob was walking in front of me in the dim light between the ornaments and a row of long broken jars: I began to realize that he liked the idea of being able to scare me.

"I think that now we can go down again" I said with firm voice. I didn't wait for him to turn; instead I turned first, reaching the creaking staircase with quite unsteady banisters.

We walked back along the corridor until we reached the hexagonal landing, (Jakob in the meanwhile had passed me again), from where we went down to the garden through the sitting room next to the library.

I thought I saw on his face a slight hesitation, maybe simulated, before he decided to show me, not too distant from the magnolia and the splendid tuft of hydrangeas, a large ring, the base of which was almost hidden by the ivy and the dense brushwood.

Jakob looked at me with determination as to challenge me, a challenge that wasn't difficult for me to understand. His eyes uttered the words that his lips, slightly lifted on the sides, would never have formulated: "Let's see if you are able to bear this as well".

His figure bent over with the grace of a Greek discobolus and without any difficulty grasped the iron ring raising the circular shaped lid with a strong screeching.

A trapdoor that I had not noticed during the previous afternoon visit (neither had Pamela shown it to me): a trapdoor that very likely gave access to underground rooms connected to the cellars of the villa. Following Jakob I went down a staircase made of iron gratings stuck into the wall.

The moldy smell and humidity was almost intolerable, the darkness almost total. Jakob had taken a lamp from somewhere and was lighting up the meanders of the underground that spread out on the right and on the left in branches, the end of which was impossible to see. Because of the low height of the ceiling it was necessary to walk with the head bent down along a trail that reminded me of a catacomb tunnel. At a certain point the space spread out into a room of more breathable air. A room that received light and air from a high rectangular split, like a glassless slit that could probably be confused from the outside with the blind windows of the cellars.

"This underground is a very beautiful example of a secret passage" I said, with extreme calm. "Where is the link with the cellars? Usually it is a lever hidden in the wall..."

Jakob was still turning his back on me while I was asking the question and I believe that he wouldn't have shown me the secret mechanism in any case, even if what happened next had not happened.

Very close to him, in the motionless and heavy air that without that single split would have suffocated us, I felt a sharp, freezing flutter of wings

Jakob turned around with a graceful movement: he had put down the lamp and put on the long black leather glove. On the wrist he was holding the falcon that stared at me with the same ferocious intensity of Jakob's look, and with its yellow eyes sparkling while waiting for my next move.

I don't know how, but I was able to keep the firmest self-control and challenged him back.

"A magnificent example of Emery" I said, while I had already identified all the characteristics of the Lanner Falcon since the evening before.

From Jakob's side no reaction. The falcon equally motionless.

"It is really time to go up again."

When I said these words, I had already turned around.

I didn't need Jakob to walk in front of me. In the dark I find my way easily, I have good night vision.

Even if, of course, Jakob could not know this.

This morning I had the confirmation that I have to compete with a hostile entity, unfortunately not without power.

The Serpent is really self-confident.

I am sure that this confidence comes essentially from her craziness.

That she is crazy there is not the slightest doubt.

What continues to be obscure is the real nature of her intentions, especially her interest towards me.

Maybe she is simply looking for a house. More than one element leads me to believe that she had not been for so long in the hotel she speaks about: it is likely that she was expelled from the Institute where she worked because of some serious fault or for showing signs of derangement.

The thoughtlessness of the Guardian, who didn't even demand a minimum of references from a stranger, is truly unforgivable.

Also, there is something morbid in her interest for me that makes her even more dangerous. If it were simply someone taking advantage, the situation would be less serious; the problem is that she feels somehow authorized to interfere with my silence. It is not clear to me if she does so with the *precise will of stopping my silence and putting an end to it – and so with a therapeutic intention – or rather to reach it herself and share it with me. As if it were possible to share the silence.*

Not even the dead can do it, even less those still condemned to life.

In any case the Serpent has ambitious aims and has found here conditions that are even too favorable.

I need to admit that she even passed the underground test with remarkable confidence, while I had deceived myself by thinking that she would already show signs of collapse in the loft.

Taking advantage of her absence, (she went down to the village with the Guardian), today I stayed almost two hours with my ear glued to the travertine of the gravestone in the garden by now visibly marked by the fall. One more time I had the sensation of hearing the Dove's voice: she was calling weakly my name, as that day in the escarpment, the last day her voice and mine resounded together.

Actually we communicated even without talking during our long walks or playing with four hands the piano or absorbed in the readings till late at night, close to the fireplace in winter, under the porch or the pergola in summer.

The word, the silence, the music were all equally meaningful forms of communication.

When we talked, no word was superfluous, every word came from the inside with a specific need, and it came up to meet with that of the other one to confirm every time the existence of the world and of love.

The same way when we played with four hands. Even more when we played the music and sang at the same time.

Silvio Raffo

I learnt from her a great deal of novels, arias of more or less famous plays, simple melodrama pieces, texts of folk sonatas.

Among the novels, there was one of Bellini that in my most remote memories gets confused with the lullabies and that actually she often sang to me in the evenings to facilitate my sleep.

Melancholy
Gentle nymph
My life
I dedicate to you

Your pleasures
Who despises
to real pleasures
born was not ...

In more recent years we sang it together at the piano and it had become almost the emblem of our union.

Since the Era of the Silence began, only that song has very seldom broken it. The words of the novel have some nights come up to my throat while half-asleep, like a weak whisper, a bit more than a moan that I wasn't able to hold back.

Other times, unexpectedly, they spurted out from the stone's heart: a spring trapped in the rock that tried to dig very slowly a furrow.

Even today from the gravestone the song reached me, more limpid than usual, crystal clear and secret as the echo of her voice that calls me in my dreams.

The Guardian and the Serpent came back from their trip in the village just when the last note faded.

I immediately moved away from the stone, struck by the absurd but uncontrollable fear that the Serpent could discover my secret.

Tonight I need to attack her in whatever way possible. I need to hurt her, before she will hurt me.

Silvio Raffo

Of that second day at the Rocciosa I remember very clearly the sensation that I felt of finally being at home.

Not only the villa, but even the village seemed to me oddly familiar. The narrow streets, intersected by alleys and stairs of worn out steps, the small stores and the poorly lit shops, jam-packed with merchandise, the wrought stone porches with roughly engraved archways, almost everything of that village reminded me of that place where I had spent the years of my orphanage. It was a village by the sea, but we very rarely saw the sea: during the group trips the nuns took us always 'under the porches' or anyway 'to downtown', and I had learnt to recognize and love the smells and the mood of the streets, of the newsstands and the markets full of colors as signs of real life, symbols of a world denied to us imprisoned.

Besides the very similar architectural structures, I found the same smells now during my wandering about with Pamela from a grocer's shop to a textiles store, from a coffee shop to a newspaper and old prints kiosk.

Pamela, who once a week personally took care of the shopping, was greeted by everyone with great respect; from the way some people looked at me, I understood that it was quite unusual to see her with strangers. For sure people wondered about who was the stranger in dark clothes and white stockings that had the honor of walking on the side of the lady of the Villa, but the thing left me completely indifferent. I savored the pleasure of that walk with a person that, among the other qualities, had the rare quality of not bothering me with vain talking and I was very happy even to carry the bags full of items.

Alessio was waiting for us in the car at one corner of the square, not very distant from the pretentious signs of a cinema-theater. While we were going back home, I observed the disk of the sun declining on the rim of the burnished top, and I felt pervaded by a wave of harmony that hadn't happened from time immemorial.

That evening at dinner Jakob seemed to be very tense. He ate staring at the plate, as if he were busy with thoughts that didn't allow any type of distraction, and never looked up at my words.

I had to overcome his fear, that restraint to open up. I had not yet tried to really get close to him, because I did not want to compromise our relation by speeding up. However, on the next day I had to start to establish a more direct relation. From a purely therapeutic point of view, I had not yet decided on a method to follow.

I thought about it for a long time before falling asleep, studying the various possibilities I had: the music, the painting, and the games (like chess, which I had seen him absorbed into after dinner).

That I was able to hold him off he did understand, of this I was absolutely sure. What he still had to understand was

Silvio Raffo

something else: that I was a friend of his and much closer than he could think of. I knew well I was running a risk, because, in the cases of narcissistic omnipotence, every attempt of approach is strictly denied and taken as an insult, but I also knew that Jakob's was a completely peculiar case to which usual schemes and the most logical predictions could only partially be applied.

The best resolution was one more time to rely on my instinct, taking advantage of the opportunities that gradually would arise.

The sleep that night was restless agitated by visions in which past and present merged together and real places and landscapes faded into the most absurd imaginary.

I was in the garden of Villa La Rocciosa, more or less where I had stopped the day of my arrival but I noticed almost immediately that the belt of statues contained in its grey grip not a house or any inhabited building, but a sort of Greek amphitheater exposed to hostile atmospheric agents. A dense and thin rain, that my body did not feel though, was pouring down from a gloomy and foggy sky. Instead of actors, on the scene there was a court of unknown characters and at the same time oddly familiar. Some were statues that had come to life (I recognized with a shiver the Venetian Lady, the Shepherd, Mercury with the caduceus and the two Sileni), others were hiding their faces but I knew that they would have uncover them the same moment I came closer to go up on the dock.

The garden had in fact changed into a court. I was slowly moving forward from the center to the stalls, as an actor who has to go on stage when the scene has already started, and my heart was beating faster at every step. One of the hidden faces was that of the Judge that ended up being the Director Miss Ida Di Pino; at her side Jakob, Pamela and Alessio looked at me with vacuous and petrified expressions.

There was also a blonde woman, dressed in blue, absorbed in playing a small keyboard. And, between her and Jakob, perched on its trestle, with indifference, was the falcon.

Rain had now assumed the violence of a storm, from which everyone though seemed to be exempt. I had not yet sat down at my place – quite surprised actually that the dock was made up by a tombstone - and I was about to pronounce the oath formula, the right hand laid down on the Bible that the Judge was handing me, when the falcon unfolded an incredibly long claw and hurt me, lacerating the flesh up to the bone.

I woke up with a start and my hand was injured.

I turned on the bedside table lamp and noticed that the back of my hand was marked by light grazes, two thin, but almost bleeding scratches. While tossing and turning, during the nightmare, I must have hit against the headboard.

I stared with hostility at the sharp curls of the wrought iron and thought that, if I had slept with a pillow, maybe I could have avoided that accident. The nuns of the Institute had got me used to sleep without a pillow and with time what was an exercise of discipline had become a pleasure.

In any case, an obscure anxiety prevented me from falling asleep again before sunrise.

Silvio Raffo

It worked.

It cost me hours and hours of concentration, but I made it.

Towards midnight, without closing my eyes, I stared first as long as possible at the first part of the last sentence, then at the wall of my room at a fixed point. After that I entered in communication with Nigro without the need of going to see it, but simply going to the tower and leaning my ear against the column of the mullioned window. I heard his calm and regular breath while sleeping, and I ordered it to act. In hypnotic state Nigro has the same and even more power than when awake.

Well, the Serpent's hand this morning had two visible scratches.

I was able to observe them in all peace during breakfast.

It was the right hand. It could be that she is also hurt in other parts of the body that are not visible.

I don't know if she understood. It is possible that she believes it was a fortuitous accident, like she hit the ledge of the bed side table and she noticed the effects only this morning.

And yet her moves this morning were somehow suspicious,

more cautious than usual. She was less confident and talked only to the Guardian, avoiding turning towards me except for saying hi.

It is also true that she regained her usual control, but I am sure that she had in her mind to entertain me with some inane and premeditated talk and that she didn't have the courage to do so.

Anyway I moved away as soon as possible, also because I was eager to write on my notebook the success of last night.

She is in my power. I proved to her that I am the strongest one.

If she follows my invitation, if she accepts the defeat - and she has to accept it in any case - she will leave today, maximum tomorrow and will spare me further efforts.

Even if I need to admit it, last night's operation didn't cost me so much effort and this game with the Serpent begins to reveal an even pleasant side.

Silvio Raffo

At breakfast I did not think it was appropriate to start a serious conversation with Jakob, also because the presence of my aunt's didn't recommend it.

I felt though that soon I would be able to do so.

A conversation, yes. I didn't hope for sure to get from him verbal answers, but a positive reaction to my approach that confirmed and strengthened the relation that was already established among us.

It was essentially necessary to set the terms of a code with him; to cancel the initial hostility and to find ways to communicate that were more congenial to him.

The favorable occasion occurred a little before lunch in the music room. I had sat down with a book in the blue armchair waiting for Jakob to come out of his room, where he had surely withdrawn to write on that red notebook from which he never separated.

After maybe an hour I finally saw his figure fluctuating in the corridor lighter than a shadow.

"Jakob" I called him with an almost imperious tone.

I surprised him. He could not do help stepping back and appearing on the threshold with a frowning inquiry painted in his eyes.

"Jakob, I would like to talk to you. Could you sit down here? " And I pointed at the stool of the piano.

He agreed, with nonchalant air, and got ready to listen as if forced to do so by the rules of education.

"What I would like to explain to you is the reason why I am here. I am a speech therapist or better let's say that this is my qualification: I have a long work experience with children hindered in the use of word both by organic dysfunction and by psychological blocks. You know very well that your case belongs to the second of these classes, but only in a relative way. You chose not to speak any more, it is not that a cerebral mechanism ceased to function. You are perfectly able to speak, but you don't want to, you decided not to want to because you are sure that there are no words that can express what you feel..." While I was going on with my talk, trying to keep the voice more still than usual, I stared at him with determination, neither did Jakob show signs of turning his look away from mine. "Thus one could ask what do you need an speech therapist for? It is clear that you need a psychologist. Well I am also this in a certain way. You should at this point of the talk be interested in the nature of my objective. You don't like that word a lot right? Neither do I. Anyway, you understand what I mean. You believe that I am here to convince you to speak, to help you to get back the correct use of the word in case the vocal mechanism had jammed... This is not exactly my goal, Jakob, or better it is not my first one or my main one..." I stopped; I had noticed that Jakob was beginning to twist nervously the hands held tight between the knees. "Wouldn't it be a good idea if you played something while I talk to you? Would you like it Jakob?"

He was very good in hiding his own disappointment, because it was as if in that precise moment I had given voice to his wish or better to his need. He controlled himself brilliantly and with the maximum naturalness he started the low and persuasive notes of a Nocturne of Chopin. From where I was, I looked at his mother watching him pleased from a black and white portrait in the middle of the wall.

"The first and main goal of my staying here" I continued scanning well the words "is to assist. You know what to assist means?" I had risen up and, standing behind him, I held back with difficulty from caressing his fair hair, rocking at the same rhythm of the notes. "Only he, who is really lonely, who has made of loneliness the essential experience of his life, knows how precious this word is. As well as he who has known through and through the solitude of a love seeking being. In your loneliness, Jakob, you need to create, and to create you need to be in relation with something or someone. Your aunt is not enough and not even the memory of your mother." I bent over the hollow of his shoulder, while the sound of the piano flew more conflicting underneath the slightly trembling fingers. "You know very well that you are an artist. You have to create, but to create communication is necessary." The last words came out of my mouth without the control of my will, and the sudden emotion reduced them to a bit more than a whisper: "I could be in some way a source of inspiration".

He stopped abruptly to play; he lowered the lid of the keyboard and rose up in order to leave the room.

"You have particular powers, in your state, I know them" I hissed implacable behind him. "But you need to understand that no one will take them away from you, even if you will speak! I will defend them with you."

The door shut up behind him with a sharp thud.

Instinctively, I turned to the portrait searching in the lunar eyes signs of an affectionate complicity.

Silvio Raffo

The game continues, it is going towards, I feel it, its main phase.

The Serpent, a little while ago, revealed her cards. She claims she wants to become for me a "source of inspiration".

She doesn't know what I am writing on this notebook, but she aspires to be a protagonist in my story.

Considered by itself, it is not an unworthy aspiration.

But in any case I don't trust her. She wants to penetrate in what I write to distract me, to guide the course of the events that concern me. The one that is moving the pen on the page right now and is well conscious of the fact that he doesn't have to stop writing before the end of the page is me, that has to be clear. No one else will ever take in his hands my pen or make me write something that is against my will because that would mean to predetermine the events not according to the agreed orders, but based on the will of a foreign element.

It is the voice from the stone the only one authorized to dictate to me the words that I write. The voice reechoes inside the sound chest of my temples for hours, it becomes vibrant memory of ultrasounds, and on these pages it gains its body and becomes transhuman.

How could the source of writing be something else?

No interferences are allowed, the thought would be irreparably weakened. I fought for more than a year in order to direct the way that will lead me to reach the only goal I am interested in: there is a still long path to cover before arriving to the annihilation of any discrepancy between will and reality.

I will never get to the state of pure thought, of the Efficient Thought, if I allow any person or entity to cross my way or to come with me on my route.

She said she knows my powers; she wants to share them and defend them from external attacks. I don't believe her.

She cannot know them, she can only vaguely grasp them intuitively thanks to that malicious nose, typical of her species – and anyway it is exactly her who represents the first attack.

What can that grotesque creature possibly have to do with an ascetical process of acquisition of omnipotence?

I don't want her, neither as deuteragonist nor as an accomplice. She claims to be my assistant, a sort of guardian angel. But it isn't clear to me for which sort of duties. Everything that I am interested in doing, I am able to do it on my own. Neither could I tolerate any type of collaboration.

If I talk about her in these pages, it is only to show how the words that I write can become, in case of necessity, destructive weapons.

In truth, I write to get rid of her.

She is only a small viper in a crack of the wall.

I could even let it collapse. In order to crush her, it would be enough that just a small part gave way. The collapse *would not compromise the entire equilibrium of the wall.*

But I still need to think over this point, ask my Good Shepherd, before anyone else, for advice.

I spent part of the afternoon with Pamela in the tower. In order to not disturb Jakob, we went up from the kitchen staircase that leaded directly in the room below the studio and had only the last flight in common with the passage from his room.

She showed me some paintings, among which a portrait of the Dove.

She had painted it in very soft colors, the features were just adumbrated and, more than a human face, it seemed like an evanescence of blue light, abstract as a dream vision.

"It is the only painting that has soft colors" I observed, "the only one in which you can feel the sense of lightness."

The other paintings had in fact stronger colors. They were almost of an expressionistic stamp.

"Malvina couldn't have been painted other than like that" Pamela replied, while she was messing about with paintbrushes around some details of her Indian landscape. "She *was* the lightness."

"I find her hair to be marvelous" I continued, indicating the cloud of blonde curls that hemmed like a crown the oval of her pale pink face.

"It was not hers. She had lost it almost completely because of the illness. That was a wig, even if no one would have ever noticed it."

I thought for a moment, oddly, to how sad and strange such a beautiful face had to be without the hair. A mother-boy, had therefore had Jakob. And immediately without a precise reason, I wondered where the wig was now. A question that was certainly not appropriate to ask.

"Your face lends itself a lot to be painted" she caught me by surprise, looking at me intensely. "One day, if you are willing to, we could think about it."

"I don't like my face so much" I replied, lowering my eyes.

"For sure it would not be the portrait of lightness."

"And of what could it be the portrait of?"

Pamela thought about it in her way that I had already learnt to know, staring at the empty space.

"Of determination, I would say. Or of faithfulness. The faithfulness of a rock."

I did not mind the answer, but I didn't think it was appropriate to comment on it. Also because she prevented me from doing so, adding something absolutely unexpected. "Yet in a strange way you look like Malvina. The structure of the body is as tiny as hers, the look has the same melancholy, and the movements are as silent as hers. There, what you have really in common is maybe the silence."

Feeling suddenly not at ease, I shifted the topic of the conversation on to Jakob: we talked about his behavior of the last two days, of those signs that his aunt interpreted as progress, clear signs of an improvement. She had noticed that he spent much less time numb against the wall, that his manners with me were unusually polite: especially she appreciated the fact that he reacted, even if just with nods, to my sporadic quotations.

All of a sudden she told me that towards evening the doctor would come: the family doctor, an old neurologist, who took care of Jakob with weekly control visits. It would have been very useful, she added, if we could exchange opinions.

I smelled the danger right away.

There were good chances that he was one of the doctors of the committee that had dismissed me from my job at the Institute.

I could have asked Pamela his last name, but I preferred not to and continued calmly the crochet work that I had taken with me in order to stay active while my partner painted.

My suspects were not unfounded.

I recognized immediately the man with the aquiline profile and pungent eyes like pins that not more than one month earlier had listened, together with other three gentlemen of the same surly look, to my detailed report on Malvina's case.

I don't know if my embarrassment was visible to his eyes. His was to mine, but it lasted only a few moments. On the other hand, I made it easier for him.

"We already met, do you remember?"

We were in the library on the ground floor, Pamela had just introduced us and I thought it was right to address her as well without delay.

"The doctor and I met on the occasion of my departure from the Institute. I mentioned it to you the other day: I had to leave the Institute where I was working because of serious divergences with my Director." Pamela followed my words with an impassive concentration, a calm immobility to which she probably had become used to thanks to the transcendental meditation exercises. "She thought some of my methods were too rigid or too ... *personalized*."

"Miss" the doctor intervened in a tone without any kind of inflexion "had to deal with dyslexic and autistic subjects, in short with the most complex, often even irredeemable, cases. I was summoned together with three colleagues to judge her therapeutic methods." His undecipherable look turned towards me. "In all frankness, Miss D'Angelo, I didn't think you were responsible ... of the disgrace. However, the Director Di Pino and two of my colleagues voted, if I can say so, against you."

Thanks to my ingrained training to repression, I managed to contain the deep relief that his last words generated in me.

"What disgrace?" asked Pamela with a shadow of alarm in her voice that contradicted the firmness of her look.

"A girl" replied calmly the doctor "that seemed to be recovered..."

"That *was* recovered" I corrected him seriously.

"The day after she regained the use of word ... she committed an inane act."

"I don't understand." Pamela's look moved from the doctor to me.

"She threw herself from the roof of the Institute" I said, feeling the absurd desire that no one ever again would ask me to speak for my entire life.

And at the same moment I saw Jakob's shadow in the hall where the last sun rays were fading slantingly.

I absolutely need to control the terror that is taking possession of me.

It is like a steel plate that gains more and more consistency inside me, perceptible physically at the height of my chest. Before she suffocates me, I need to suffocate her.

I have already become acquainted with the evil power of this icy grip that grasps and doesn't let the prey breathe. I experienced it for an incredibly long time last year when I had to accept my mother's abandonment.

The chilling moment, the one when terror began and at the same time touched the highest peak, was at the funicular railway.

Neither I nor she had noticed the breach on the ground, a square hole in the grey surface cut by thin cracks like those that arabesqued the icy lake on which we had skated many winters. Even that one was supposed to be a happy walk, like all the innocent raids of two children longing for discoveries.

When I saw her falling down swallowed up by space, I became familiar for the first time in my life with the grip of terror.

It was as if I were paralyzed but the desperate need

Silvio Raffo

pushed me to action and guided my steps. Going around the disconnected platform, I went down the escarpment with a lot of effort. The roar of stones that had accompanied the fall had not yet faded away when I arrived at the ditch that had received her body on the edge of the precipice. The crushed stone that fell on her was hiding her body almost completely to the sight: only a strip of the blue dress and the white shoes revealed her presence under those implacable rocks. The most voluminous rock was exactly the one that was covering her face and her shoulders, and maybe had already destroyed one of the most perfect masterpieces of nature.

I felt on me the weight of guilt. Not much for not seeing in time, with the physical eyes, the source of danger, but for not having protected enough the happiness of the years I spent with her, defending her with the complete concentration of thought in order to direct the events in our favor.

The terror of absence, of irremediable parting, was my mate from that day on until I understood, through a dazzling flash, that it depended on me to found again the bases of our life by defeating even death.

Under that large immovable rock, my mother's voice called many times my name, and my voice, that in return called hers, had not to pronounce a word ever again. Only this way she would be able to come back.

The terror that visits me now is of a different nature and, if possible, more cruel.

I was achieving the improvement of my exercise, the fulfillment of my recovery operation and something (someone) wanted to prevent it. Shortly I would have been entirely in control of my will and my will in control of Thought, *but that horrible woman interfered with me and my goal.*

She is an assassin.

I don't have the least doubt that she intentionally caused the death of that girl, after forcing her to speak.

I know I don't have to fear that she will succeed with me.

I need to write it in clear letters: she will not succeed.

I need to regain piece and control, both necessary for my defense.

Unfortunately the truth is that no one is on my side (no one among those alive): the doctor, that dull man, arid like wood and colder than a Prussian General, even expressed his respect for her and gave me a speech of an aberrant nonsense in which words like faithfulness *and* collaboration *were repeated in a disgustingly exhortative tone. As far as the Guardian is concerned, she is also caught by the morbid charm of the Serpent: it seems as if, in all these months, she had been waiting for nothing else other than her arrival.*

The so called reality of facts is that, in the short time of two days, a situation has been created that undermines the foundations of a structure that was built over more than a year with patient and disciplined constancy.

The terror that pervaded me doesn't have to weaken the strength and the coherence of my thought, or it will be my ruin.

With the thought or, if more efficient, with concrete action, I need to destroy the Serpent.

There are two possible ways to be followed. Either I eliminate her, in fact, directly, or I try somehow to unmask her in front of the Guardian's eyes without leaving any doubt, forcing her to accept the true nature of she who claims to be my assistant: *that of a mad criminal that has in her blood the*

Silvio Raffo

bent to kill and has chosen me as her next victim.

The fact that Jakob had heard our conversation in the library worried me only at the first moment: later on thinking about it, it seemed to me correct that he knew the whole truth.

After the talk that the doctor had with him privately and that lasted not more than a quarter of an hour, he withdrew to his room, where he stayed also for dinner. To the repeated calls of his aunt he replied with two sharp and nervous knocks on the desk that in his code meant a resolute no. I convinced Pamela not to insist and Alessio took care of serving him with his usual imperturbable behavior.

Later on, before withdrawing for the night, I knocked on his door, resolute to talk to him with sincerity.

"Jakob, open please."

I had to wait some moments, but he obeyed. He was still finely dressed, but his face was devastated and his hair ruffled. He inspired me a tenderness even more yearning than usual, of an intensity that I had felt only with Malvina. On the other hand, since the first moment I had seen him, I had realized that that boy would have been in control of my heart as only she had been before.

98   Silvio Raffo

His room had light pale blue colored walls and was full of books and discs, arranged tidily on shelves and bookcases. The bed slightly curved, like an alcove, was reflected in a golden framed mirror that occupied the space between two shelves of the bookcase. At the sides of the big triangular window, someone – quite likely Jakob himself - had painted two huge eyes of a very intense blue that oddly struck me.

I sat on the only armchair present in the room, next to the record player. Jakob, who sat down at the desk, at the corner of the window, kept his eyes low but stayed on guard. I had never seen him so marked by fatigue and so upset: it was clear that he was waiting for my next move.

"I know perfectly well that today you heard everything, or anyway the main part of the talk." His back had a slight start. "I came here to complete the subject by adding some details. It is right that you know my event entirely since what you heard this afternoon was a fragmentary report that could mislead you."

Jakob straightened up, shook his hair back and looked at me coldly as to invite me to go on.

"The person that is really responsible for the death of that marvelous child is my Director. She had always been jealous of the very strong bond between me and the little creature, as on the other hand she had always envied my abilities, gifts that her arid and obtuse nature had irremediably denied to her. The day after the recovery of my protégé, or better after her decision to come back to a dialectic contact with who was around her, that woman forced me to take an afternoon off." While I pronounced this word, the look fell on a book whose title was exactly *Escape from freedom*: I just noticed it because similar coincidences had already occurred an incalculable number of times. "As if I had ever needed it! I never knew what to do with those so called off duties. Anyway I was forced to it. The girl was used to my constant presence, and that shocked her. While I was wandering like an idiot among the paths and the gardens of a public park, she went up to the terrace of the solarium and threw herself headlong into the courtyard."

Jakob covered his ears with his long white hands, but I knew he was listening.

I went closer to him; I bent down and with my lips grazed his scented hair.

"And I also need to tell you that the name of that girl was Malvina, Jakob. The same splendid name your mother had."

His body reacted as if crossed by an electric current. The waves of his hair decomposed in a vortex of stormy waves, the tense figure moved away from the desk and stood up in front of me with all his power, almost threatening me. Horror was painted in his eyes. For a moment I thought he would hit me and maybe I wished he would. Instead he stood motionless staring at me for another very long moment, and then he covered his face with his hands and threw himself on the bed, while short painful hiccups began to shake him.

"Everything is ok" I told him bending on my knees at the edge of the bed. "You will win. I know it for sure."

Our bodies were at a minimum distance from each other. I was controlling with difficulty the shiver that had taken possession of my body.

Jakob stopped almost immediately to sob and when I left he was still crouched down in the position of a fetus as if sleep had already taken possession of his conscience.

"Don't you understand that it was your mom to send me

Silvio Raffo

here?" I whispered from the threshold without knowing if he would hear me. "I am a humble maid of your Dove."

Silently I closed the door and leaned the forehead on the wood. I felt exhausted but I didn't know what exactly had taken away all my strength.

It is very difficult for me to write.

Terror is innervated up to the hands, the articulation of the joints becomes oddly difficult, and the fingertips tremble as if fallen in prey to a delirium attack.

But I will finish this page as well.

It is impossible that this won't happen.

The Serpent has profaned my room, daring to come close to my person; she crawled up to my hair and whispered impure things.

The dead girl, that is the girl she murdered, had the same name as my mother.

My mother would have sent here the Serpent.

After she left, I noticed that the watch on the wall had stopped and that a book had fallen down from the shelf on the left of the mirror. With the breath taken away from the terror, I picked up the volume of the Bhagavadgita bound in black leather: I needed to absolutely check the page on which it had opened. I would have liked to avoid that check. Before seeing it with my physical eyes, I knew already what number it was. The number that is chasing me since always. The number that I don't dare to write down here, because

Silvio Raffo

malicious thoughts become incarnated in it.

I find it over and over everywhere, in any occasion that has to do with numbers: it is the sum of the numbers that form the date of my mother's death, it appears with obsessive frequency in license plates during my seldom walks in the village, it camouflages or openly reveals itself on the covers of records or inside my books. The most dreadful effect is that obtained by the basic number repeated three times, but even simply the pair is a sign of trap and danger.

I don't know how I found the strength to close the volume of the Bhagavadgita and put it back on the shelf. I kept saying to myself that I had surely left it in an unstable position (in fact, I had looked it up a few hours earlier), and that its fall had been purely fortuitous.

But how was it possible, with all the good will of this sad world, to consider a pure coincidence even the fact that falling down it opened right on that page?

It was then that the trembling began to shake violently my body from head to foot. I threw myself again on the bed and pressed the ear on the wall asking for the stone's help.

At the beginning the howling of screech-owls, particularly insistent, disturbed my hearing, but little by little I began to feel the familiar, reassuring and light breath that came up to calm down my anguish, from which in about an hour I might have been destroyed.

Now the trembling is not convulsive any more, only some hints remain that I am able though to control.

However, terror will not be defeated so easily and only if my strength proves to be, as it should, superhuman, I have some hope to succeed.

There is not the least doubt that that horrible creature

is an emissary of the evil. If I could ever have had some reluctance to accept this terrible truth until tonight, her words and the events connected to her entrance in my room force me to surrender.

There is a negative force, unfortunately very strong, to which the idea that I reach the control of the so called reality is intolerable. A hostile entity, that tries to hinder my power of shaping through the writing the world that surrounds me.

She even tried a few moments ago to make my fingers numb, contracting them with shivers and pangs to prevent me from taking the pen again and writing.

It is not completely clear to me the reason of this hostility, since the only field where I would exercise my omnipotence would be that of my private life, without setting for myself any type of competition with what regards the facts of the world, which I am not interested in at all, and essentially without bothering anyone.

Why can't I be left alone?

What does this hostile force exactly want from me?

Maybe very easily the goal I aim for is something forbidden to human beings. Men are condemned to be inferior beings. The enemies of these exercises aimed to reach omnipotence are the lowest and the gloomiest expression of the human thought. These enemies fight against who they want to rise for pure envy so that power will not be held by an intelligence freed from mundane ties, but continues to be submitted to rules of the most sinister brutality.

But in vain I make an effort to obtain a logic explanation for evil. Evil is blind, it loves darkness for the only and very simple reason that it is incapable of seeing the light.

It is important anyway that the positions have been

Silvio Raffo

clarified and parts have been identified. I didn't want the disagreement, I would have avoided it and I wasn't even interested in the hypothesis of a victory on something or someone other than me. In short I didn't consider mine a path where I would run into friendly or hostile travel mates.

But if she wants war, war it will be.

Writing has helped me a lot, it gave me back the usual lucidity and, as I feel I can say right now, a kind of reasonable peace.

The Serpent was almost able to make me scream, not more than one hour ago.

The evil effects of her visit have even threatened the exercise of writing.

However, I was able to elude both dangers, and I notice furthermore that I wrote one of my most important pages.

Terror watches over, as the enemy does.

But my power is stronger.

I will trample on the Serpent and her infertile poison will die out on the impassive stone.

The next morning Pamela insisted on beginning my portrait.

In my whole life it had never come into my mind to be portrayed by a painter, I had never had the occasion neither the desire. But it was difficult to deny something to Pamela.

For the first pose she chose a corner of the pergola: I was sitting on a green bench that turned its back on the nymphaeum, while she had set the easel between the gate and the bench in front of mine.

I was wearing the grey apron, with a white collar and a row of oval amethyst color buttons that came down to the waist; in my hands I had my lace work, a *valencienne* lace handkerchief.

Almost immediately, at the mullioned window of the tower I saw Jakob's slim figure stretching out his right arm to throw the falcon in the air. To that gesture followed a long guttural sound, very similar to a bird's sound that seemed to give more impetus to the flight.

"Nigro is his only friend" Pamela said, already absorbed in her work. "He trains it in a very particular way, but not violently. Jakob hates any form of violence on animals, the only exception being the grass snake. He got it used to plundering all kind of objects: gum rabbits, stones, a ball, and small fabric puppets. He built some even of wax."

"Aggressiveness is not reduced this way" I pointed out. "On the contrary it is preserved and developed to the highest level."

"It has happened only seldom that he let it catch some other bird or some rats. But in those occasions he was clearly disgusted. He personally takes care of feeding it, sometimes with Alessio's help."

"It was the animal's torment from an aesthetic point of view that nauseates him: he cannot tolerate any kind of disharmony." My eyes were looking in vain for Jakob's shadow that had disappeared from the tower's room. "You know that your nephew is an artist, just as his mother was." ("And he himself is a piece of art", I added in my mind.)

Pamela nodded.

"I have always known it. What I wonder is if that will be his salvation or his ruin."

"Pain is something that is necessary for him. A condition that is essential for him in order to create. I believe that Jakob will write something great. If he hasn't already done so."

For a moment, I felt the weird sensation that my words were turning against me as a strident echo: as if I had said something that had been better kept silent about.

Pamela began to speak very slowly again.

"No one can touch his notebooks. I know that some are locked in the first drawer of his desk, of which he hides the key who knows where. He never separates from the red one and I believe that he writes daily on it. I don't know what it contains."

While she was speaking, she drew quick and firm strokes on the canvas, scrutinizing me obliquely with her eyes at times almost rapacious.

"There are moments when your look is so similar to that of Nigro, did you know that?" I told her keeping my immobility without any effort.

She smiled with bitter indulgence.

"I don't think I have ever exerted my aggressiveness. It doesn't seem to me to have any, not even a gram. My spirit is too contemplative. If you exclude meditation, only painting really satisfies me."

"As music for your niece and writing for Jakob."

Even if it didn't seem appropriate to me to name him, it was inevitable to include in my thoughts that mysterious character that had created Jakob, the Sculptor, who populated lastingly his absence with so many sinister creatures. In fact, almost all arts were represented by members of that extraordinary family, whose destiny had called me to be a part of it, me so completely lacking of any creative gift.

It seemed to me that Pamela had read my thought.

"My brother was the only exception" she pointed out. "He has always been indifferent to any artistic form. On the other hand, politics and high diplomacy completely absorbed his thoughts and his interests since he was young." She gazed into space with a vaguely sad expression. "Even when he was here, he was never really with us. And now his homeland is India."

"A country that you love a lot, it seems to me."

Her look came back to life.

"It will seem weird to you, but only there I feel that I am

really myself. The air that I can breathe there has something so vital and primitive, that I cannot find anywhere else. Those desolated plains, the low sun on the Ganges, the gardens... Have you ever seen an Indian garden, Verena? It is like a tangle of spells. The nature's breath is something like what had to be the perfume itself of the ground the instant immediately after its creation."

Without doubts I would have deeply disappointed her if I had told her that I did not have any interest in the Asian countries, that I had never traveled in my life and that I did not feel any desire to do so. My universe seemed to me suddenly inexpressibly narrow and flat, but it was right this, its monolithic closure that brought me closer to Jakob's solitude and this was one more reason for me not to regret my decisions.

As if I had called him pronouncing his name loudly, Jakob popped out that precise moment from the corner of the porch, almost running, wearing the black fustian suit. His hair, with its coppery shimmers, sparkled on his wide and straight shoulders. He gave us an indifferent look that could have been taken as a vague sign of greeting, and went out from the gate onto the path, as hurrying up for a meeting.

I knew that on the crag, a few steps from the surrounding walls, his ferocious friend, trained to abstinence, would land in a short time, shaking the dark wings. But I didn't know with what prey.

"Today I will take him with me for a walk" I thought loudly. "He feels much better than yesterday evening."

Whatever the Director Miss Ida Di Pino thought, I was still convinced that shock treatment would always produce the best effects. Sure, I had been a little abrupt the evening before, and Jakob's tears had cost even me a deep pain, but no one could have denied that this morning the boy seemed to be blooming again.

The same had happened with Malvina, when I told her the truth about her birth that had always been hidden from her.

"Truth" was repeating even now a voice inside me *"the most precious of all goods."*

With this page begins not only a new chapter of my notebook but also the crucial phase of the Era of the Silence, the one on which I am sure depends the final outcome of my exercises and of all my efforts.

It is necessary to move from theory to practice.

Mankind, as Goethe teaches, feels fulfilled not as much in the introspection as in the action.

My writing is already itself a concrete act, but too many times I allowed imperfect feelings, like fear or uncertainty to affect its innermost power of determination.

What I write here will come true only if I load the word really with its fullness and let be what the word means.

In this operating process, some rules become necessary as is obvious: for example, I shall never use again verbs in the past tense in the main sentences. Only the present and the future will be my tenses from now on. It is very simple to understand: the writing presupposes a modification of the so called real, an incision in the plot of the events. Or rather, you can say that nothing is that hasn't been written: isn't the divine creation connected to the word (which in the case of the Almighty doesn't need to be written but isn't even *properly pronounced)? The Greek term* logos *shows in an exhaustive way what I mean: word-thought. But I don't want to waste my time in trivial philosophical discussions.*

Word produces facts. If that is true, as it is true, from now on my speech will be simply a pre-writing of the events.

I don't have the presumptuousness of being able to determine them with the pure thought because I am not God: I need to use the writing and I am very pleased to do so.

So. The madness of the Serpent will be revealed to the Guardian with indisputable proofs: I will set up the first proof through tonight's simulation, studied in the least details.

I don't want though that this episode, whose outcome cannot be other than positive, to cause the Serpent to go away, because I have in store for her another more direct and, so to say, more personal and definitive surprise.

I know very well in fact that to limit oneself to sending her away from the Rocciosa would not be a sufficiently safe solution.

For the other project that I will hint at in the next chapter in order to not compromise the success of this one, Nigro, on which I can blindly rely, will help me.

Soon the Serpent will come and ask me to go out for the walk that she suggested, or better forced to, already at lunch.

Unexpected things are allowed.

Only those in my favor, of course.

Silvio Raffo

Pamela didn't want me to have even just a quick look at the sketch of my portrait; in the afternoon after some quick touch up, she wrapped up the canvas in a plastic covering and put it in a corner of the hut.

At lunch I noticed that Jakob was quite tense although he tried to look at ease and relaxed. Tension was all inside him, as if he were making a plan from whose elaboration he could not get distracted, not even for a moment.

When I suggested taking a walk, he agreed with an almost too natural indifference. I myself tried to be careful in not showing the least enthusiasm.

Around four o'clock, as we had arranged at lunch, I knocked at his door. He opened it almost immediately; he had put his hair up in a small ponytail and the features of his face stood out brighter and more harmonious. His beauty, as much alive as unreal, caught me once again by surprise, causing in me an almost painful pang that pride tried angrily to suffocate.Even later, while he was walking in front of me - I let him choose our destination – I forced myself to look at the burnished landscape showing the first shy autumn's marks. However, his agile and proud body, resolute in his solemn gait and impatient with anything that was accompanying him other than his own steps, prevented me to take my time to look at any other object.

From the main gate we had turned into the wider path, the one that Alessio, causing Pamela's smile, called *the avenue*: at the junction, as I had foreseen, we went up the rocky ridge of the mountain leaving the village behind us. A little further a quite worn out yellow arrow gave the directions "To the Springs": at that second junction the road was suddenly going down again. Here the road had a sidewalk on which you could see disorderly aligned a long raw of jars and bottles. I remembered the stream that Pamela had mentioned the day before and I understood where we were headed to.

A basin shaded by age-old evergreens welcomed us at the end of the descent, beyond two sumptuous lavender flower beds that a sign strictly prevented us from touching. The prohibition though was violated with elegant innocence by an iridescent butterfly that moved from one flower to the next without ever stopping. I pointed it out to Jakob who turned briefly his head and even rippled his lips in a hint of a smile.

We sat down on a stone bench in the almost cold shade of huge limes and oaks. Water spurted out, arrogant and light, from the mouths of small tigers sculpted in the rock. Few tourists came up to the fountains with bottles and filled them carefully.

On other benches, scattered asymmetrically in the valley, were resting old couples and foreigners with a dreaming air: the peace was absolute, scanned by the water roar and the light rustling of leaves.

"That was a great choice, Jakob. Thank you."

Silvio Raffo

Words struggled to dig a way to come out, but the steady tone was not showing my emotion. Besides what Jakob was giving me was too precious for my gratitude to be verbally expressed. During those moments I even understood, as no one else could have, the supreme coherence of his state, the sublimity of his silence compared to which any word would be like a grotesque sound, a banal profanation.

There was anyway a message that I had to communicate without breaking the spell. I put my hand close to his, which was resting on the stone, but without daring to graze it.

"Jakob, I want you to know this: I understand your value, the same way I understand your pain. Where I need to take you is the defeat of fear, much more than the reconciliation with the word. Your enemy is inside yourself, you need to free yourself of it before it dims your mind. Your mind needs to stay clear and in control of its faculties in order to perform its job which is to create."

He stared at me but almost expressionless, while I was uttering those broken sentences, making me feel like a ridiculous defendant in front of the implacable court of his eyes. I was not sure if it did make sense to continue my speech, but he ratified its conclusion by standing up abruptly from the bench.

Instinctively without thinking of the possible consequences of my action, I grasped his wrist and held it tightly.

"You need to tell me if you understand. If you believe me."

He had a shake, similar to dizziness: he looked incredulous at my hand clawed at his thin wrist, as caught by a horrible vision that had nothing to do with him. He controlled his anger, I think, because of strangers being around, to whom he would never show anything else than decorous.

"Tell me Jakob. I order you."

His face was an iron mask, but he lowered it in an affirmative nod. Only then I let his wrist free: my fingerprints on his skin seemed to me for a moment the strip of a seal and I thought rather inadequately that with Jakob I wouldn't have any hesitation to draw up a blood agreement.

On the other side of the valley we came up back to light on a winding path, bristling with briars. Jakob had resolutely taken it and was already halfway up the slope. Back on the ridge of the steep slope, we followed the trace hardly visible of the path that became more and more steep and rough, running at times along the overhanging escarpment.

Jakob was advancing almost running, challenging me to keep his pace.

"Don't run!" I yelled at him almost laughing, as if it were a childish game, although I was out of breath.

Suddenly he stopped and he turned around, with two widely open eyes, bewildered and burning with a wild glare. I had to stop my run abruptly: for a moment I lost my equilibrium and with my foot I caused a large and flat stone to roll down to the valley. At the same time, not very far from Jakob's back, I saw the shape of an abandoned building from which two ominous black iron wheels with rusty and almost burnt gears were sticking out.

Jakob was still staring at me and madness was portrayed on his look.

My voice rose severe, and steady as my intentions.

"Stop it Jakob, it is vain. Don't pretend that you want to kill me. You have to stop it with these performances."

As a reply I got a look full of scorn and I felt clearly the tension that it was costing him to get back the coldest self-control. In fact he succeeded and turned his back on me, returning to walk at a natural pace.

The weird thunders that accompanied our walk back towards the house lasted the whole evening. The distant roars, echoing from a sky that stayed clear until sunrise, were followed by as much unjustified flashes when the darkness came down: as in a theatrical scenery, you could only feel the external symptoms of the storm, and only the representation of the event was being performed.

Even after dinner, at my window the lightning renewed its flickering premonitions at longer and longer distances. Since more than an hour the two bright triangles, corresponding to Jakob's and Pamela's rooms, had stopped to be reflected in the segment of the garden between the magnolia and the corner of the tower. At midnight I stopped reading, as an old habit, and I turned off the light.

Immediately after, I heard a sharp and violent thud coming somewhere from the garage, as if something had been thrown from above and had touched the ground in that instant.

Without turning on the light, I jumped out of bed and ran to the window of my veranda. The nymphaeum was lit up as I had never seen it before and on the edge of the pool was laying supine Jakob's body in his light blue silk pyjamas.

I had the sensation that the walls of my room were closing on me, and similarly the floor and the ceiling seemed to swallow me up in a vortex, while I was running towards Pamela's room, tripping over my own clothes. For the first time in my life I entered a room without knocking at the door. Waking her up took some precious, maybe wasted, minutes. I screamed something probably incomprehensible and we went down as two mad women through the first staircase on the back.

When we arrived out of breath at the nymphaeum the lights were turned off and there was no body lying on the edge of the pool. The little stone elephants were dozing indifferently and when we turned on the lamps the blue water did not reveal any prey.

Pamela looked at me upset, with her long white braids frayed on the trembling shoulders, while I was repeating like an idiot: "He was here, I saw him!". A thin rain had begun to pour down and, as to seal definitely the joke, a beat of wings flew in the dark air very close to us, accompanied by an acute and scornful screeching.

It was Nigro. For a moment I thought that he was about to attack me; but it slipped away almost grazing my face, and went around the house from the side of the tower.

We went back up in silence, without calling Alessio, whose well-known deep sleep was another element not in my favor. On the first floor the door of Jakob's room was left ajar but not locked.

Entering we found him sleeping peacefully: the right arm in a tangle of light blue silk was holding tightly the pillow on which his cheek half covered by his hair was leaning.

His breath was calm and more than regular.

Silvio Raffo

The success of tonight's operation guarantees me a parenthesis of relative peace that doesn't have to become inertia.

I can at least devote myself to the preparation of the next plan with a peace that I wouldn't otherwise have.

The Serpent is in a state of prostration that maybe she has never known in her life and will struggle to recover from it. But it is contrary to her nature to give up and she will not admit it, not even this time.

The reasonable choice of spontaneously going away could save her, but she is far from taking that direction.

It is alright for me because I know that, even physically distant from here, she would still continue to try new contacts, and to disturb me with inevitable intrusions.

Nor do I have to be moved by the sadness of her state. I know that she doesn't go out of her room and that she doesn't come to throw on me her poisonous insults only because she is still under the effects of sedatives that Alessio and the Guardian gave her more than once. Since she has never taken medicines or tranquillizers in her life, she will be dazed or maybe even feverish for good part of the day.

I am sure that the Guardian doesn't believe her story and that she thinks, exactly as was in my wishes, that is was a hallucinatory episode.

Her trust in the Serpent deteriorates now, shortly she will be sure that she made a serious mistake by welcoming in her home a mad visionary. She will reconstruct in her mind the event of the girl forced to death and will think about the best way to get rid of an assistant totally incapable of being useful to my case.

I want things to go this way, but at the same time I know I don't have to give up my second plan.

It will be the Serpent herself to force me to do it and in this I feel with chilling certainty that our wills are the same. Her bent to self-destruction is as strong as her goal to hinder me.

I, instead, want only to win the game. I know that only by winning I will obtain the only reward I am interested in: no more no less than the reconstitution of the Being through the Thought.

Since too many hours I don't hear the stone's voice any more.

It is as if something were holding me back: an absurd, unjustified fear. I don't have to fear that the voice could dissuade me from my plan. On the contrary it will give me precious advises.

At the end of this page I will go down in the garden. I won't do wrong neither to the Dove's gravestone nor to the Shepherd's pedestal: I will give myself equally and with the same pleasure to each of them.

Silvio Raffo

I slept for an excessive number of hours, a heavy and unnatural sleep. At the same time, it was as if I was awake.

Images of Malvina and Jakob came in my mind, one on top of the other, hazy, with persistent obsession, at the threshold of a numb conscience on which the dark sense of regret and of bitter and fatal impotence lay heavy, like a lead blanket.

Malvina, Jakob and an abyss underneath them. An abyss ready to receive their bright forms to dissolve them into nothing. Malvina was also strong and beautiful, her body slim and graceful as a palm or hazel sapling ...

I was awake by now, but those images vivid more than ever were printed in front of my eyes as perfect illustrations of the *motto* on which I had dwelled on while reading the evening before: "DIES YOUNG WHO IS DEAR TO THE HEAVENS".

Suddenly and almost blindingly, it was revealed to me how peremptory my disgrace was: my horrible fate of being the witness, maybe an unintentional author, of the execution of that cruel sentence. The only desire of my sad life had always been that of relieving the pain to my little friends and fate condemned me to assist instead to their destruction, maybe even to cause it myself. My premonitions, my extrasensory gifts, of which I had been so proud, did serve to nothing else than to favor death.

I was the maid of the abyss that demanded for itself the young innocent victims of a cruel and perverted god. Sure, the scene could change: from a white terrace, blinded by the sun of August, to a wretched courtyard punctuated by formless marks - or from the veranda of a country house, at night time, to a delightful nymphaeum blue marble watched over by four small stone elephants...

But Jakob did not die.

The blurred memory set properly the last plug of a mosaic, whose final composition contradicted the desperate vision of the previous picture.

Jakob did not die. He had only faked to throw himself from the window of the veranda to simulate, and only to my eyes, his own suicide.

Why did he do it?

Conscience regained lucidity as if the leaden veil that had obscured it until that moment had been suddenly dragged away by an imperceptible gust of wind.

Jakob had set a trap for me with the only purpose of making me look like crazy in front of his aunt's eyes.

He had foreseen everything in the least details: the precise hour I turned off the light, the lampposts lit up only for me to illuminate the nymphaeum, me going down from the first staircase on the back while he would come up from the tower side and the faking of the most innocent sleep with the pyjamas perfectly dry since he had only put his hand in the swimming pool, while he had kept his body on the edge of the pool.

With what had he caused the sharp and heavy knock that

Silvio Raffo

made me jump out of bed? The imitation of the sound of a body falling on the ground had been perfect: it was the only piece of evidence that I was missing, but I didn't doubt that I would find it.

The great relief that had given me the certainty of knowing he was alive was now being substituted by a discouraging desolation: Jakob had deceived me.

Jakob wanted to hurt me.

The bitterness of disillusion was burning inside me as a wound. But I needed to be strong.

I rose up from bed and moved a couple of steps towards the window, feeling like a tightrope walker that advances with lots of uncertainty on his first rope. Overcoming the dizziness and a slight sense of nausea, I managed to draw the curtains of the window that was looking onto the garden. The daylight – a pale and empty light, of a sky just clear of rain – could not tell me precisely the time, but I was inclined to believe that it was already afternoon.

The first image I saw, right on time like an obsession, was that of Jakob crouched down on his mother's gravestone.

My heart sunk: the scene I had in front of my eyes was really the Statue of Love. With her, with his Dove, Jakob would have never been able of a thousandth of the ferocity that he had shown with me.

Maybe it was exactly this to upset him: that I in some ways was assuming towards him a maternal behavior. That I dared even think I could substitute the Dove. But wasn't it maybe logical and natural that I tried to give him back the lost certainty of being loved, and the support of a faithful presence?

He wanted his mother back. Nothing and no one else

could win over his love. The silence itself he had chosen as a rule of life was a strategy that allowed him to prolong unconditionally the relation with her and in some ways to renew it.

I, who didn't know what a mother was, maybe was not able to completely understand.

Yet something told me not to give up. A silent and obstinate voice, similar maybe to the hiss that Jakob believed to hear from the stone's heart, on which he leaned his ear, forced me to try again because the salvation of that ferocious soul, whatever it would be, depended on me.

I put on my clothes and put my hair up with the slow and mechanical movements of an automaton; with the same stunned heaviness I went down to the ground floor.

From the kitchen I heard the quiet voices of Pamela and Alessio. The servant was talking about the beeswax that that year was unexplainable scarce and his tone seemed quite worried. I felt the sensation of being still sleeping and listening to those voices in my dream.

They were both very kind asking about my state and offering me immediately warm tea, but in her eyes I thought there was the shadow of suspect. We went to the library and the first thing that I thought of saying, surprising first of all myself, was that I wished to leave the Rocciosa.

Pamela didn't get upset and her answer was as much unexpected.

"Verena I think you have to stay. If for nothing else then to allow me to finish your portrait. There is nothing else that bothers me more than to leave my work half finished."

I agreed to pose and in common agreement we chose the tower. I was wearing the grey apron of the previous day, and

Silvio Raffo

therefore it was not necessary to go back to my room and get changed.

We met Jakob on the stairs, but I avoided his look holding tight my wrists to give me strength. It was very weird what was happening to me: as if a sudden, unknown indifference had taken possession of me and froze my will. The almost unreal suspension of sounds, space and time in which it seemed to me to be floating with no physical consistency, was making me perfectly docile to a kind of fatalistic apprenticeship. I wasn't even interested in knowing if Pamela believed in my story or if she was on Jakob's side. I didn't even talk to him at dinner, but I held a casual conversation with Pamela on the most advantageous method to choose to grow orchids.

My lace work was at a good point and I devoted myself to it sitting peacefully on the softest chair in the living room. Even with the windows closed, in the absolute silence I was able to hear the sad and melodious concert of the last crickets: it was a gentle echo that gave me comfort and seemed to persuade me to a peaceful resignation.

But later on, in my room, when I was already persuaded of going to bed with my book, an unexpected and violent impulse that I couldn't stop pushed me towards the desk.

The pen was flowing fluidly and fast on the white paper of a scholastic notebook.

Jakob what you did had neither sense nor beauty. You need to accept to be loved. It is not for my will that I feel so close to you. I know everything of you. I even know what you write on your notebook, as if I were writing every word with you. You won't win the next duel. You need to win a quite different fight.

I didn't even reread what I had written. I crossed the corridor stealthily and slipped the note under the last door from which was still filtering a ray of light.

From the inside you could hear being played the low and whispered notes of a romance that I recognized immediately.

But my mystery is closed in me
my name no one will know ....

I was very surprised by this new coincidence, because the *Turandot* had been my favorite opera since my childhood. Going back to my room it was natural to me to think about Jakob as the princess locked in her tower; and challenging the smile of scorn that my Director would have reserved for me, I couldn't avoid seeing myself as Calaf who at sunrise would win.

Silvio Raffo

Once again, the Serpent tries to undermine my position of superiority.

As I predicted, she comes back to attack. The hard blow she suffered last night couldn't have other consequence, after the brief dizziness, than that of increasing the poison of her gall.

Her tactic is now that of a false insinuation in order to create confusion in the enemy and so the desire to give up.

In her sneaky and agitated message, besides using with vulgar arrogance the verb to love, she reveals even to know the content of this notebook.

It is clear that I don't have to give any importance to her words. I know with absolute certainty that she cannot have read these pages.

The very seldom times I don't take the notebook with me, I put it in the drawer of the desk and no one knows where I hide the key before leaving the room. To dwell on the hypothesis that this afternoon I left the drawer open due to a reprehensible oversight seems to me simply morbid. It is such a mechanic action, the one of opening and closing the drawer, that I don't even remember if I did it – I mean today

- and I don't intend to go along with her plan wasting time and energy by asking myself this question.

In any case, her allusion to the notebook is by itself a very serious insult. I won't allow it to upset me but I cannot even allow it to go unpunished: essentially, it does only reinforce my decisions.

It is a dark night, obscured by shapeless clouds. The sky is empty: a muddy blanket subtracts the moon and the stars from the sight.

An anonymous night, esthetically insignificant.

I don't want a night like this for the time when the Great Reunion will take place: there must be a strong and bright moon, worthy of the face that it will light up.

These dark and worried days will not even be a memory. The memory itself will be erased because there won't be anything to remember. Time and space will gain back their pure dimension in the unlimited expansion of an eternal moment in which silence and music will merge.

Today my Dove's voice seemed sad to me: it was maybe the fluttering of her wings in the stone's heart, as in a very slight intermittent arpeggio, that blunted the words in a vague moan.

The Shepherd's tone instead was more resolute and his message more explicit: faithful to his pragmatic belief he invited me to action, urging me to finish as soon as possible.

I don't think I will disappoint him. He doesn't deserve it.

Besides, not much is left before the end. All the material I needed has been put together without any difficulty; only some, let's say, formal details are missing.

I am confident; actually I am sure, I will beat the Guardian on time. Although she is usually very fast.

Silvio Raffo

The morning after I woke up very rested, with the sensation of having recovered all my strength.

The sky had the color of lead and a shadow of haze covered the garden; the walls from which the statues stood up more pale and grey than usually, like pure forms without weight, seemed to me oddly fragile as if next to an inescapable crumbling.

Pamela requisitioned me in the tower to continue the portrait that I had not yet been allowed to see. She had her usual intent and grave air, and for a moment I thought that at the end of that work, that day or the day after, she would tell me that I was free to go. Deeply inside me, though, I didn't believe it and a maybe unjustified peace had overcome any anxiety.

Quite soon the falcon began to circle around the tower. Jakob must have been in the garden but from my position I couldn't verify it.

Nigro was shaking its dark wings, streaked white at the edges, causing a sharp and annoying noise, and continued his circle as in a spectacular exhibition reserved just to the two us. Suddenly it stopped and disappeared to our sight, gliding slantingly: I heard clearly the premonitory hiss of the attack.

When it reappeared I saw that his claws were holding a whitish object, not bigger than a ball. It was only for a moment, and then it disappeared again, although I had not heard any call.

"*Horus*" I remembered loudly, in a sort of excited, hypnotic fervor "the falcon of the Egyptian pharaoh that serves his master from distant."

"It is incredible what Jakob is able to make Nigro do, both according to and against his nature" said Pamela keeping concentrated on her work. "Not only does he make it capture any type of object with the stimulus of food, but he has also trained it to very difficult exercises. They have a special code made of specific sounds: at a whistle, at a breath, at the snapping of Jakob's fingers corresponds every time the execution of a precise move by Nigro."

I kept looking at her almost dazed: it was as if suddenly the eyes of my mind had opened widely and light had turned on, but the image that it was illuminating was not yet visible.

In the afternoon, still feeling that strange sense of anxiety, I went down to the village on my own. I had to do some trivial shopping, but in particular I had to find an appropriate gift for Jakob

It was absolutely necessary to disarm him, to convince him of the groundlessness of his suspects in my regards. My prostration of the day before had to be enough to reassure him of his power (no one else had in fact ever reduced me to that state), but also not to encourage him to further attacks: that I had been vulnerable maybe had been positive if it succeeded in making him understand that I was a friend

Silvio Raffo

of his, who in some ways needed his help as much as he needed mine.

In a shop at the beginning of the porches, with the window packed with confusedly assorted merchandises, I found what I was looking for: a puzzle of hundred pieces of delicate colors, mostly rose and light blue that portrayed a mother and a very small son in the center of the painting. The kid was distended on a hammock and the woman, wrapped up in light veils, watched over him lovingly; behind a cascade of wisterias, a grove studded with bushes of hydrangeas let tiny lanterns and strange creatures, like elves, and unicorns, shine through.

When I came back, I found Jakob sitting at the table of the room where I had seen him the first time only four days earlier, numb as a mortally wounded beast. He was absorbed in the reading and, even if he had certainly noticed my arrival, he didn't raise his head nor did he move a single feature of his face. His profile had the grace of a crystalline statue and at the same time the peremptory incisiveness of the marble.

Overcoming the senseless and frustrating shyness that was threatening to pervade me, I put the bundle on the table.

"This is for you Jakob. I think you will like it."

He couldn't ignore me any longer, he stayed perfectly calm and didn't show the least emotion, while his white hands opened the package with the same elegance they had when grazing the keyboard of the piano.

I am sure he was struck by the fineness of the design, also because the figure of the mother, blonde and slim, surely had to remind him of his adored Dove. With an almost imperceptible nod and an oblique look he thanked me; then, going back to his book, he let me know that he considered the meeting finished.

Halfway on the corridor, I noticed that the door of the room next to that of Jakob was half open. Maybe Alessio or someone else who had gone in for who knows which reason had forgotten to close it.

Instead of going left, I turned towards that part careful of walking as silently as possible.

The Dove's room was the only one of the house I had not yet seen and I didn't see why I shouldn't take advantage of that occasion. There was a slight chance of finding someone inside, but I rejected it immediately: it was too silent and besides no light was on.

The room was slightly smaller than Jakob's and mine (our rooms, situated at the extremes of the corridor, were the only two that had a view on both sides of the house); the rose antique wallpaper, still perfectly preserved, and the curtains of a warm cream color gave the room a tone of delicate intimacy. The bed was in the style of an alcove, as Jakob's one, almost completely hidden by crimson velvet clothes and a huge mosquito-net like curtain. On the dressing table shelf, in front of the mirror with three panels framed in onyx, I saw three objects aligned, as for an exhibition, very close to each other: a blonde wig with slightly wavy hair, a pair of big sunglasses with white frames and a silk scarf with rose patterns.

I didn't even touch them because I felt spied on: as if Jakob's eyes, as big as those painted in his room were piercing my back. It was such a strong sensation that I was forced to turn around. There was no one on the threshold, of course, but my anxiety persisted, so I left the room giving

Silvio Raffo

just a quick glance at the portraits on the walls.

The corridor as well, dark almost as during nights, was deserted. I hesitated in front of Jakob's door asking myself if it was the case of trying a patrol even there. The risk that he would catch me in his room scared me less, actually the encounter could have been useful. In particular I was interested in getting close in some way to that notebook... I felt that, whatever its content was, it was of almost vital importance to read it, as if the secret key of our relation and furthermore of our destiny were hiding in that notebook.

But as I suspected the door was locked and I had to give up.

It was him who came to me that night.

I saw him playing with Nigro in a big meadow that surrounded the Rocciosa, dismantled miraculously of all its statues. He had unusual, joyful manners; he jumped and whined, amusing himself with a swing rope that all of a sudden became a whip. After some whistling whipping, to which Nigro responded with elaborated circles, he turned with resolution towards me. Only now I noticed his outfit: a coat of raw cloth, sewn all together, that gave him the odd looks of a nurse; in his hands he was holding a mask protected by a net. Coming towards my still body, he was staring at me with a smile no longer childish, but mocking and evil. The weirdest detail was that Jakob *passed through me*: his body, erasing every resistance of mine, proceeded inside and beyond me as if I had no physical consistency.

Even without turning around, I saw that now he was going towards Alessio's beehives where he stopped for a long time to put the mask on his face.

I woke up with a start, bathed in sweat, and prey to the

most humiliating embarrassment. At the triangle of the window the pale lights of dawn were crawling in.

The Serpent is changing tactic. Her current state of disadvantage suggests her, as a Latin author would say, to turn to more mild advice and plays even the card of the emotional complicity.

Her gift, a puzzle of rather cheap quality, has some grace from an esthetical point of view though: the picture is quite corny but likeable, especially thanks to the background where the surrealistic overcomes positively the sentimental.

I think I will be able to recompose it in less than an hour.

I don't need to fear to slip up by enhancing the value of her gift: the fact that I devote myself to a diversion by her suggested doesn't give her any real reacquisition of power. Actually it will only be in my favor because the Serpent will think of my compliance as an act of mildness towards her and this false thought will make her be more disarmed for the next attack, which will also be the final one.

I don't want in any case to hurry up. Even if the purely material work has been completed, the training exercises need at least two more days and I want to improve them with the utmost care.

If I think carefully about my last year of life, on the

specific nature of the Era of Silence, I notice that its essence can be summarized exactly in the concept of exercise. In Greek, the most artistic language, the same word – askesis - indicates both the concept of exercise and that of ascent or improvement. What is asked of me is exactly to pass the tests, to refine myself and to make progress in a trial. Nor could I on the other hand reach my aim, to what even in military language is called victory, without fighting any battle, or without testing in some ways my strategies.

I found out only a short while ago that the value of trial is fed by one of its secret lymph: the pleasure of risk. The daring itself would be sterile boastfulness if there weren't any consequence to be paid while pursuing a high task.

I admit it; I owe this discovery to the Serpent.

Now I can understand what I didn't understand: why she crossed my path. Exactly to allow me to measure my powers, to exercise them and to show her that they are superior to hers.

She wants to see beyond my screen and is interested in what that screen is hiding for an ambition of omnipotence. I know that the detail that mostly struck her in my room is the painting on the sides of the window: what my mother, while she helped me to refine them, called very accurately the eyes of Zeus.

The Serpent would like to have those eyes instead of her pale declining splits: to see what those eyes can see. Because of this as well, she burns with the impure desire of reading my notebook.

She even tried to force the handle of my door. The eyes of Zeus saw her while she was messing about awkwardly in the dim light of the corridor.

Silvio Raffo

That she reaches these pages is what cannot and will never happen.

There is no access for her, if not in just one sense, to the story that is here narrated or better to the life that is here written about.

Here the circumstances and the ways of the Great Reunion are getting ready: she, who blindly desires to hinder it, cannot do other than favor it in spite of herself, with the total resignation to her crazy intentions.

The sweetest memory of my days with Jakob goes to the afternoon of the day after.

Sitting at the table made of stone under the pergola, with his head slightly inclined and the lips open, he was putting together the pieces of the blue mosaic with the attention and the care of a scholar absorbed in an exam test. Not distant from him on an old wicker chair, I was finishing my work as well, slowing it down in order to not finish my design before he had arranged all his pieces.

The still mild summer air had light fragrances of wood and the shrill songs of the last swallows could be heard. Letting myself go to sentimental and maybe futile daydreams, I was imagining Pamela painting us in a painting named "Jakob and Verena" or "The rest", and that it would be the sweetest and most delicate of her paintings.

With perfect synchrony my lily got the final touch when Jakob completed his picture by setting the mute and contrite face of the unicorn in the bright foliage. Raising his head, he tied the hair with his usual gesture. From the corner of his eye, he sent me even a sign of invitation: he wanted me to look at the completion of his work.

I rose up from my place and stood behind him with the lace work still in my right hand.

"You were very good Jakob. I finished at the same time as well. " I showed him the flower, embroidered in such thin wefts that it was hard to distinguish its form.

He stiffened, making it clear that I was too close and that it was starting to disturb him; I moved away immediately, conscious that the level of confidence we had achieved a few moments before was anyway an exceptional result and that it didn't have to be absolutely spoiled.

The chance to not withdraw in a humiliating way was given to me by Alessio, who right then appeared at the corner of the porch with the grey coat that he used for his work at the beehives. Controlling the dismay that caught me by seeing him dressed as Jakob in my dream, I asked him if I could walk with him, and he was slightly surprised by my request.

In about an hour I came to know everything you can know about the life of bees. Probably it was the only subject Alessio was not reluctant to talk about. Although there wasn't much to be seen, being the season of the hibernation already begun, he taught me all the tasks that kept the bees busy from May to September.

While I was listening and observing his unusually animated face, there was a moment when it seemed to me to lose the notion of time: with impressive brightness I saw in front of my eyes the images of a short movie that more than thirty years ago the nuns had projected in the large room of the Institute on the life and the activity of ants. From the cloudy and heavy veil of the oblivion, my visual memory dug up the frames that, when I was a kid, had struck me the most: those concerning a particular quality of worker ants that didn't reproduce themselves but were devoted to precise tasks. Who knows for what reason that destiny had particularly touched me.

"It has been an unusual summer" was Alessio saying, shaking his head. "We didn't even have one queen. The workers worked a lot to elect a new one." He dwelled for a moment, checking inside some glass containers, and frowned. "Another thing that I cannot understand is why so little beeswax was obtained."

As during the conversation with Pamela the day before, I felt pervaded by an apparently unjustified excitement: even Alessio's words, pronounced so naturally, gave me incomplete but alarming signs, allusive to truths that I had to discover, that regarded me so closely. As sinister shadows that challenged the peace that had just been established between me and Jakob.

I would have gotten the answer to both my questions and one more time the confirmation to my premonitions in one single moment: in what I could call my descent to the Underworld from which I was still one day and two nights distant.

Of these two nights the first one, unexplainably sleepless, brought me to a new discovery: at a certain hour Jakob, maybe as a habit, left his room and the house.

During his absence (first I had heard a light shuffling in the corridor, and then I saw him from the window walking in the garden towards the magnolia), I went into his room of which he had left the door ajar but not locked. Although I searched carefully everywhere, it was impossible to find what I was looking for, and the desk drawer stayed inviolated. A strange voice was whispering that it was better this way and that to force it would have been a sacrilegious act other than an absurd one.

I was very careful in not leaving any trace of my visit and didn't stay there for more than a couple of minutes. Jakob instead didn't come back until one hour later.

The morning after a telegram from India arrived: Pamela's brother was informing her that the celebrations for his thirtieth year at the embassy were going to be three days later.

Pamela could not miss the jubilee.

In the page from where the new phase of the Era of Silence has taken place, I had decided not to write ever again about events regarding the past, but I have to report what happened tonight.

From two to three, while I was busy with Nigro's training exercises, the Serpent was here.

I have indisputable proofs. The watch on the wall stopped at two twenty and the only other time it ever stopped was when she came to visit me in my room.

Besides some books on the desk have been moved and my pencil case is not at the usual distance from the lamp.

I made the unforgivable error of not locking the door, relying on the fact that the Serpent was sleeping: at exactly midnight her light turned off as usual.

Clearly she had already the intention of spying on me.

I am sure that she didn't find the key of the desk drawer. So as I am absolutely sure that I closed it yesterday evening. Or maybe am I writing these words to convince myself?

To reopen the door to doubt, to hypothesize even just remotely that she might have put her hands on this notebook would mean losing all the advantages achieved in the last

Silvio Raffo

days.

Exactly what the Serpent wants in order to reinforce her powers.

Already the fact that she forces me to use a past tense to comment on last night intrusion puts me in contradiction with my purpose: the past tense makes me lose ground as even a kid would be able to understand.

To retreat, at the point where I am now, would be the same as to be ruined.

It is not possible in any case for her to win. I have too authoritative protectors to be possibly intimidated by the tricks of a Serpent: the Shepherd, the Dove...

"Mild as doves, but clever as serpents."

Why does the voice from the stone insist in reminding me this evangelic warning?

It is as if implicitly the qualities of my mother and those of the woman who tries to take her place by stealing my powers were given the same value.

With her I need to go on and fight, availing myself of her own weapons, as on the other hand I have done since the beginning: the weapons of astuteness and deceit.

The most favorable conditions for the final encounter are being prepared: the Guardian has even been called back to go to India. Her brother, that man, who I have seen only twice in my life and who has never been interested in me nor in my mother, wants her with him for an abstruse and memorable anniversary. She will depart as soon as possible, maybe even today: on the other hand she was looking forward to go back, for her whole life she has desired nothing else than to be in India, she has been detained for years and years in the prison of the Rocciosa only by her distorted sense of duty (first my mother's illness and then mine). It is not excluded that this time she leaves with the plan of arranging with her brother her permanent accommodation over there.

She is not yet completely convinced that the Serpent will not be able to help me; intimately, she thinks that she is an odd subject, quite interesting from a psychological and esoteric point of view. It is true that, after the other night episode, she is not succumbed to her charm as before and is very uncertain about believing her or my innocence, but prefers as always to wait before any judgment and in any case to leave me with her.

She is too tired to stay here, India is calling her and here with me there will be a nurse specialized in desperate cases: destiny gives her free rein and she will follow its signs.

If one excludes the almost inexistent presence of Alessio, I will stay here alone with the Serpent.

The oblique lines of her horrible eyes will try again, and with more and more sneaky intrusions, to spy inside my reins.

I will prevent her from doing so in the most radical and extreme way. After that, no obstacle will ever again interfere with the Great Reunion.

Silvio Raffo

Pamela didn't lie by saying that she wasn't in the habit of leaving her works half done.

My portrait was finished before noon. The telegram had arrived that morning very soon and she was going to fly that same evening. She had already told the news to Jakob and showed some kind of perplexity at the idea of leaving us as she told me with frankness.

An impulse that surprised first of all me pushed me to an ambiguously reassuring assertion: "You need to be relaxed. There won't be other episodes like that of the other night and I feel perfectly able to take care of Jakob."

The look she gave me resembled that of our first meeting: deep though distant, it communicated a sense of extreme, resigned solitude and at the same time a sense of disillusioned fatalism. No matter if she believed in my version of the faked suicide or that I had been victim of a hallucination, she considered in any case the events of that night now over, and of negligible relevance.

"I recommended the doctor to come and check Jakob as much as possible. You can consult each other and it will be good for both of you. I don't think though I will stay away for more than ten days." She drew back a couple of steps and heaved a sigh of relief. "So, Verena, your portrait is done."

Finally I could see myself: with the almost anxious and distrustful curiosity of who doesn't like to look at herself in the mirror because she doesn't have a high opinion of her own image, I looked at that pale and angulated face, with strongly severe features that the brush had highlighted with cruel persistence. The line of the lips was slightly open in a sad hint of a smile. The long and of Asian cut eyes, instead, were sparkling with a green icy light, and they were the strong points of the entire portrait. The black braids put up in a *chignon* around the head: the high-necked dress and the lace work that could be seen at the height of the bent arm completed the image of a child prematurely withered, from the nineteenth-century, in who I had actually always recognized myself.

Those eyes, though … They were too bright not to lead into the suspect of a secret passion that right from the strictness of discipline and chastity received the deepest nourishment.

I had the sensation that with that portrait Pamela wanted to send me a message and that the message was to remain the way I was.

For the entire afternoon Jakob stayed in his room. At lunch he kept the usual mask of poised impenetrability, but a shadow darker than usual veiled his intentionally inexpressive look. Pamela talked to him for a long while and from the corridor I heard more than one sentence: if on one side she was giving reasons for her departure with lots of details, almost as to justify a sin, on the other side she wanted to ask him sincerely if he thought that the reasonable alternative of him going with her was really an impossible thing.

Silvio Raffo

While I was observing, without seeing it, the old print of a cricket game, I imagined Jakob's quick and sharp refusals, his wavy hair, and the limpid and proud look, averse to resentment that was reassuring without comforting. I felt the love knot that, not yet undone, was binding him to his aunt but I also felt between the two the barrier of an impassable border.

She left with the garden, half-sleeping in the already evening shade, and with the statues of the Dioscuri, at the sides of the gate, as backgrounds: Alessio had finished loading the bags on the sedan and Pamela was hugging Jakob, who in his rigid immobility seemed more fragile than ever.

She gave me a hug as well; I felt the hard contact of her cheek and the delicate sandal perfume of our first meeting.

"I will think of you Verena in my Indian garden as a special plant."

Jakob and I stayed motionless at the gate until the car disappeared beyond the junction of the path. When the roar of the motor was not even an echo anymore we were still there, a few steps one from the other: almost stunned by the sudden and total silence, we realized that we looked exactly like two statues, as the ones that were above us. The only difference was that we were not the sons of any divinity. Or at least we had never gotten any official certificate.

I felt a strong emotion growing inside me, coming up as a wave. Jakob and I were alone at the Rocciosa. Would our night reins finally establish an agreement between their surly kings?

At the unreal light of the lantern, I saw a flash of real terror flickering in the eyes of my partner: he was the first one to shake himself from the spell that challenged to petrify us. His body was pervaded by a rapid shiver; he turned abruptly and, almost rushing off, he crossed the garden and went back inside.

I followed him as an automaton. An unknown and savage force was burning inside me.

Jakob took the stairs, hurrying up his pace.

It was like a chase, for who knows what competition or aim. A show that could appear grotesque, if there had not been behind us, not yet revealed, but almost visible, the demon of destruction.

Jakob reached in a flash the door of his room and locked it.

I called him in vain, screaming his name in an imploring invocation that if I had been more lucid would have deeply humiliated me.

He didn't reply. How could I hope for the contrary? I heard that he was barring the door with an armchair.

I let myself fall down in the corner of the corridor, the same way I had seen myself in my dream the night before my arrival at the villa.

I barely found the strength to get up and go to my room at the other end of the corridor. The huge deep blue eyes of an irritated divinity were piercing my back as sharp darts.

Silvio Raffo

I need to take action as soon as possible, this same evening.

I think the Serpent wants to kill me.

I mean in a direct way, with her own hands.

I realized it just a few moments ago, at the gate, after the Guardian's departure. Her madness reached the climax and no one can do anything to stop her.

I am sure that her hands would have the strength to strangle me.

The only thought of feeling on me those claws, of which she already dared to let me feel the slimy caress, causes in me the most unbearable nausea.

I am not even interested in understanding why she wants to kill me. On the other hand who can inquire with clarity into the mind of a mad woman?

She chased me up to the door that I took care of barring with the most heavy armchair (with other two chairs I also blocked the entrance from the tower side). If she had reached me, I am sure she would have strangled me without delay.

Even if her ambition is preferably to let people fall in some abyss. Maybe she would have thrown me then from a window *or from the top of the stairs.*

The idea of calling that obtuse doctor is not even to be considered because I know too well that just one infringement to the rule of silence could be lethal as much and even more than a direct attack of the Serpent.

What I need to do is simply to stay locked in here and try to calm down. In two, three hours at the most, Alessio will be back (the Man of the Bees is also a very efficient driver; the distance from here to the airport is not more than hundred kilometers and the roads at this hour of the night are empty).

She won't be able to break down the door; she will have to accept to be powerless. The most likely hypothesis is that she is already in her room; gradually the fury attack will calm down. If I stare at the point on the wall above the right eye of Zeus, I can see her: she is already lying in her bed. I don't have anything more to fear.

As soon as Alessio will be back, I will take action and I will have to do so paying the greatest attention to any detail.

Her sleep is light and I will take care of interrupting it at the right moment.

Things will go in the best possible way.

In any case, this notebook will be the only reliable evidence of how events went and the tangible proof of the superiority of my power to foresee the future.

Silvio Raffo

A strange flashing light woke me up before sunrise: a small beam, or a torch, was turning on and off at intervals, as if an agreed sign.

I had fallen asleep not a long time ago, after hearing Alessio coming back and parking the car in the garage. It wasn't difficult to locate the top of the tower as the place from where the light was coming. A sign... who could it be if not Jakob, who communicated with the reality only through his code of gestures and signs instead of words? Was it possible that he had finally decided for peace, an agreement to resolve the situation, and wanted to put me to test, first of all with a message to interpret?

I put a cardigan on my night gown and went out, without even putting my hair up.

The darkness of the corridor began to disperse in the first light of the day: the frames of the prints projected oblong shadows on the walls. In the loaded and suspended silence, any little noise would have had the effect of an explosion. I could have taken the stairs above the kitchen, but instinctively I chose to exit from the side of the garden and then go up again. I was so worried that I didn't even think about checking if Jakob's door was closed as I had left it.

Downstairs, the living room next to the library was reflecting in the mirrors the elaborate forms of the chandelier and of the silver vases. The French window was locked, and the shutters were half-closed. From there I went out into the biting and livid air that was still struggling to receive the weight of light, and went up from the small threshold of the tower whose chain, as I imagined, had been unlocked from the inside.

What I found in Pamela's studio was only my portrait set on the easel, in the middle of the empty room. It was as I had seen it earlier, but immediately a different detail stood out that affected the entire image: the eyeballs had been filled with white; hurried and violent brush strokes, unworthy of Jakob's elegance, had completely erased the effect of the emerald green and the oblique cut declining on the sides.

My face had been transformed into a horrible mask of dazzling vacuity.

The same light that had woken me up appeared again in a reflection from the window behind the painting; at first I thought it was a reflection, then, getting closer to the mullioned window, I saw the glare again turning on and off in a point in the garden between the magnolia and the gravestone. It seemed the renewal of a nightmare, but in spite of the anguish that had pervaded me at the sight of the disfigured portrait, I felt that I would be able to face any other test. If the evening before it had been impossible to reach Jakob and to force him to a confrontation, now he wouldn't be able to escape from me again.

I went down through the small spiral staircase with cautious steps. I felt there was no need to run, actually what was

Silvio Raffo

asked of me was control of every movement and absolute lucidity.

One more time the statues caught me by surprise. It was certainly the icy light of dawn to make them so spectral, yet it seemed to me that in no other moment the cruelty of their smiles could have been more real: the Sculptor had created those fauns and nymphs exactly for the light of an autumn's dawn.

The torch was laying on the grass of the garden a few steps from the ring of the trapdoor; the lid wasn't fitting on the base, but had been removed and the entrance to the undergrounds was half way open in front of my feet, as a little abyss that I could not have seen. For precaution I had picked up the torch and the descent to the Underworld was relatively easy.

Without the torch for sure I wouldn't have seen with such clarity neither the bag nor the wax doll: one almost leaning against the other, they were hidden, together with two big black nets, in between a shelf and the corner of the wall of the first entrance hall otherwise deserted. I noticed to the touch that the content of the bag was sand and immediately I seemed to hear the muffled thud of three nights ago: of course Jakob had hung it on a rope or something similar, tied to the railing of the veranda, that Nigro had broken at his master's sign, while he was already laying on the edge of the swimming pool.

The doll had been a stroke of genius, if not cleverer surely crueler: Jakob had reproduced on it the features of his face with admirable care to train his winged partner.

The real prey this morning was going to be me.

Even if my blood had frozen and terror had paralyzed my

limbs, I wasn't surprised by hearing the lid of the trapdoor being closed. I knew by now with absolute certainty what would happen.

As soon as I heard the hiss of the falcon, I crouched down in the space underneath the shelf and threw the doll on the floor in the next room, in the vicinity of the perch. Unfortunately it hit the sharp edge of a settle and it broke right at the height of its face. Nigro, who had come in as bullet from the vent, lashed out at it without delay: I heard first the shiver of the wings and then the violent break. But it might have been disorientated by the disunited pieces because it didn't even touch them. Besides, it was directed somewhere else. Now the falcon had to substitute the bee wax with human meat: even more than meat, a couple of eyes with a sight almost as perfect as its own.

It was quite quick in finding me: I heard it searching, scratching and then stopping in not more than three points at the same distance from the center of the undergrounds; then, hissing stronger than when he had come in, as if gone mad with fury, he threw itself against my face.

It managed to wound my right eyelid. But I was faster and wrapped it up inside the double net and with the torch I stunned it until that deafening clamor was made silent.

Silvio Raffo

What I am beginning to write is very likely my last chapter. It is not a coincidence that the notebook has almost reached its last pages.

Not everything went as in my prescriptions. I had to take that into account since I didn't follow rigorously the rules of writing. But I consider myself the winner in any case. The powers of the enemy have been neutralized.

For a long time the Serpent won't be able to see.

She is lying down on the bed with bandaged eyes.

The mildness and the compassion that this morning the Dove begged for her were respected: that the execution wasn't complete certainly depended on my mother.

After closing the lid and going back to my position behind the gravestone, I ordered Nigro to go back to his den to plunder the Serpent and then I leaned my ear on the stone. The messages that I perceived almost immediately were an invocation for mildness and a meeting for this night.

I would never have dared to hope that the hour of the Great Reunion would be so close: on the other hand, what obstacles will interfere with it now that the Serpent cannot see?

Only now I realize that in a certain way I have to be grateful to her: her coming to the Rocciosa, thanks to the implicit threats of destabilization, favored my apprenticeship of omnipotence and accelerated its improvements.

In this sort of trials, no stimulus is more fruitful than danger.

The message that I received this morning cancels any possible doubt. Not even times have importance any more. I know that past and future will merge tonight into an undifferentiated present.

The past is nothing more than a hazy shadow, a succession of fragments that foresee tonight's event: some of these fragments are still of consuming tenderness, but any future that dismissed them as simple memories would be a misleading betrayal. They will never be memories because, already at the time when I lived them, they were not part of time. Some moments, when my mother and I went up silently along the paths of our hill or played the piano with four hands, they were not part of time. For a privilege given only to the few who are meant for it, we could savor, during our daily life experience, the secret sense of Eternity.

That sense of Eternity that starting from tonight, after the Great Reunion, will become our only reason.

Something we could not have talked about during those moments when we anticipated its pleasure, so as I am not able to talk now that I am about to take final possession of it.

The imperfection is not in truth but only in our language.

If it has always been vain to talk, from tonight on it will be vain even to write, because there won't be anything to be determined, nothing to define, and nothing to create.

What else should I create or want, in fact, after I will be

Silvio Raffo

reunited with the creature that I myself took away from the gloom and brought back to life?

As the desire and as the deceitful spiral of time, even my writing will end.

Lying on the bed with bandaged eyes, I thought again about my descent to the Underworld and my climb back.

It had been quite exhausting to find the passage from the undergrounds to the cellars, with the bleeding eye and in my state of mind, but persisting in feeling the wall my hands finally met a bulge similar to a rough chain, rising which the wall had literally transformed into a door. From the basements I took the only possible stairs, tripping over the big steps made of stone that went up as a spiral, and from the entrance hall I managed to get to my room without crossing Jakob.

I medicated and bandaged myself with the tools of my personal first aid. The wound was only a light one.

What worried me now was the decision that I could not avoid about the behavior to keep with Jakob. That he had wanted to really eliminate me, even to deprive me of my sight, was a reality I could not doubt about.

If I wanted to be faithful to my usual methods, I would have to face him, to repeat to him that he had to give up these absurd war plans, which were destructive first of all for himself, and to convince him that I was not the enemy he had to destroy, but that the enemy was right that part of him that armed him against me. But I felt that this time a direct attack would be unproductive, and that I had to leave to Jakob the initiative of doing the first move in order to calm down his upset soul: paradoxically, I would get from him the advice on the way to follow to cancel his resistances.

I had to let him believe that I had been wounded more seriously than I really was, or at least to fake my capitulation. In a short time he would have shown me the best way to proceed.

I stayed in my room for the whole day, I asked Alessio to serve me lunch making up a trivial fall from the bed and recommending him to tell Jakob that I wouldn't be able to take care of him until I recovered. I aired even a possible admission in the hospital if I didn't show signs of improvement.

In the afternoon the sky finally cleared itself of the clouds. The leaden blanket that weighed on the mountain since the previous day gave way to a pale candor that made me think of the delicate shade of the Dove's eyes.

Jakob had to be in his room, absorbed in writing.

Sooner or later I would have in my hands his notebook and even if it seemed to me that I already knew its secrets, no joy would ever equal that of discovering the features of his handwriting that I imagined to be clear and slightly engraved as a precious decoration on an old parchment. I felt suddenly the innocent desire of sharing with him those pages, of alternate myself with him in the draft of a piece of work that in some way would bind and go beyond our person.

Because I was sure that he was writing something great: a poem, maybe, or the novel of his Silence.

When the evening came, I had not received any sign yet.

The immobility was by now unbearable. When Alessio served me dinner, I asked him about Jakob; he replied that the young master had been in his room the whole day, exactly as me.

I had pricked up my ears for hours, but I didn't hear his door open when he went out because he chose exactly the moment when I was talking to Alessio to carry out his purpose.

A little later, I saw him in the garden.

The moon was almost full and illuminated with an oblique cut the statue of the Shepherd, the gravestone of the Dove and a good part of the well. I had been very careful in not turning on any light and I am sure that he didn't notice to be observed: he crouched down with the ear on the tomb; I saw his wavy hair sparkling when it merged with the stone.

That was the sign. For a moment of extraordinary intensity I felt his head on my breast and felt the effect of a violent brainwave. Something pushed me to leave my room, but from the corridor, as had already happened three days earlier, I was called back by the half-closed door of Malvina's room.

Jakob left it always open, maybe as a memory of a child habit. He must have been in there earlier today and before going out.

On the shelf of the dressing table, I saw exactly as the other time the blonde wig close to the big dark glasses and the scarf.

My hands were moved by an automatic force; I did every move with extreme naturalness but in a hypnotic state that maybe could be explained by the suspended and hazy inertia

Silvio Raffo

of the entire day spent in bed between wake and sleep.

The wig fitted perfectly, the dark glasses didn't obscure the sight, and the blue scarf suggested a dress of an appropriate color: the light blue one on the first raw in the closet, whose tears had been lovingly mended.

When I looked at myself, the mirror was reflecting three women to me equally unknown.

At this point I had to check Jakob's moves. He wasn't in the garden any more, unless he had hidden somewhere not visible from here. The risk to meet him at the wrong moment or in wrong place was big, but my steps guided me independently on my will to the lower floor.

I will never know if Alessio noticed me passing by from the kitchen: I know that I arrived easily at the stairs next to the library and from the French window I saw clearly Jakob's figure between the pergola and the nymphaeum. He was walking with his dance step towards the gate of the Sileni, leaving even that one open as a silent invitation.

While following him, I was very careful in staying behind him in order to not be heard or seen.

I knew very well where he was going to and the faith that the moment of his liberation was coming closer overcame any possible fear: the signs that were leading both of us to the completion of our efforts were too clear. His suffering had always been separated from mine, but in a little while, seeing me, he would relive that terrible moment and thanks to me overcome it.

I made him gain space, sure that he would go to the funicular from the main path. I took a path that was going up for a short way, and then surrounded sideways the massive cubic structure, clanged in its three layers to the rock like a gigantic crab. I popped out on the lowest floor of the building that, like a huge terrace with no railings, looked directly into the vacuum; the skeleton of a rusty and crooked staircase was leading to the higher layers; the steps were shaky and I had a hard time with keeping the equilibrium.

I finally found myself in front of a platform, slantingly lighted but very clearly, like the stage of a theatre with lunar scenery. Jakob was seated on the edge of the field that was like a border behind the hill: he had his face bent on the knees and was concentrated on the waiting.

I didn't call him. I remained motionless, on the side of a huge toothed wheel, waiting for him to raise his head.

The surface that separated us was flat and porous, similar to a fallen wall: here and there emerged bushes, pieces of railways and gears that untied like serpentine volutes.

Everything happened in a flash.

Jakob put his hair back, he saw me, screamed again and again one word with the most limpid and sonorous voice that I had ever heard and rose up to run towards me.

The breach in the floor swallowed both his body and his scream.

I heard a roar of shifted stones that rolled down to the valley.

I went down along the escarpment, tripping over between briars and crushed stone, up to the gorge in which he had fallen. From there I lowered myself on my back towards the bottom.

It wouldn't have been an easy task to find him in that dark crater, but his voice reached me, he was repeating in a joyful moan that same trembling word.

When at the end I lowered myself on his body immobilized

by the stone, I was careful in not calling him by his name, and I only grazed his hair.

He had found his Dove again.

But it was me, Verena, the one his voice had called mom.

Thoughts crawl along the frozen walls of the mind as emotions once did along the soft walls of the heart.

Not all of them have the same tenacity or consistency: some are little more than a light shiver that soon extinguishes, others penetrate with insulting violence there where the surface is less smooth, less protected from assaults; and others just give advance notice of themselves, full of possibilities, without ever taking shape.

They have crackles like dry wood burnt by fire, or remote pulsations like ultrasounds.

In fact, they are silent: they neither find words, nor lasting reason.

They are water snakes that attempt an impossible climb, basilisks defrauded of their ancient privilege that wear themselves out in the frustrating mirage of rehabilitation.

They don't know seasons, or climates, or tiredness; they don't prefer one particular moment to another. Time does not concern them. Also, time is just an unpronounceable and insignificant word, a fictitious abstraction.

At the Rocciosa, maybe, time never existed. This vitreous sky, more silent than a desert, has always weighed on the

Silvio Raffo

corroded but indestructible walls by the force of a spell.

Since almost two days now he, who tries to rip a word off my lips, has the sensation of being in front of an impenetrable ice wall.

On the other hand what I found is something too absolute to be able to translate it in words.

My thought can maybe be summarized by a single sentence:

"I will not say how short Time is because it was revealed to me by lips that were immediately sealed and what is open respects what is closed".

Neither the doctors nor the men in uniform that take care of the so called investigation, nor the Guardian of the Tower, when she will be back, will be able to get even just one word from me.

I will stay perfectly silent, right here where I am, in front of the mirror that reflects three images of me equally motionless: blonde hair with a light copper-colored shade, dark glasses with white frame, and pale blue dress.

The only visitor whose presence I can tolerate is Nigro. Even this morning he came in from the half-closed window and sat on the column at the side of the bed: perfectly docile, like a perfect accomplice, it watches over my secret in a silence of stone.

The fact that that man arrived here at the Rocciosa should bother me, but I am realizing that it leaves me completely indifferent.

He says his name is Klaus and most likely that is true.

He is the Sculptor, the man whose address I found in the drawer of the dressing table

I don't know who called him.

He says he is Jakob's father.

A completely meaningless assertion. And yet he said it, pronouncing those absurd words in his foreign accent with a hoarse and unpleasant voice that came out through the thick and greyish beard.

I looked at him only for a moment, but it was enough for his horrible face to be indelibly stamped on my mind. A face without humanity, contorted in a grimace with scorn, very similar to the statue of the Shepherd, in which maybe he had meant to sculpt a self-portrait.

What does that fellow want from me? With what right did he settle here twenty years ago and even more offensively on this day that should be devoted to silence and veneration?

How can he pretend to be the father of my creature? Jakob never had a father, exactly as I never had carnal exchanges with any type of men: he was born from my thought and only to me he owes his life. That same life that he physically lost in order to be reunited with me in Eternity.

But even this is a truth that I don't have to and cannot reveal. I still find it hard to believe that that disgusting man dared to speak to me.

As if it was even remotely possible to get an answer from me.

My only and last words are these that I am writing here.

Jakob who has begun this notebook allowed me to conclude it.

The key for his drawer was hidden in the right eye of Zeus, in an almost invisible recess of the wall, where the border of the eye thickens in a stronger turquoise shade. He himself made me find it the other night when I came back home and

Silvio Raffo

of course I will put it back where it was after ending the page and I will lock the notebook in the drawer.

No one will ever find it. Our story will be kept unknown to the world, secret as Jakob wishes it and how it should be.

I know that sooner or later they will take me away from here; it is inevitable but even this it totally indifferent to me.

That man uttered a word that is obscurely familiar to me, and that was then repeated more than once, in a reassuring tone, by the so called family doctor.

The word is Institute.

I hear it reechoing insistently and crawling on the walls of my temples.

What a strange sound. It brings to my mind a pale and bony woman, bandaged in a grey apron, a woman with flat and oblique eyes similar to those of a serpent.

Moulehorn - Brusino
July-September 1991

About the author

Silvio Raffo was born in Rome in an aristocratic family. He lives in Varese where he is a university professor. He has translated nine Anglo-American poets, including Emily Dickinson's work for Meridiani Mondadori. He has written ten novels, including *Voice of Stone*, finalist at Strega Prize. He has published the Gozzano Prize winner *Lightings of the Vision* and other collections of poems. He is the author of the play *Pas de deux* (Jean Vigo Prize) and critical essays on various authors of the Classical age (Plato, Seneca, Marco Aurelio, Greek lyrics) and contemporary period (Antonia Pozzi, Amalia Guglielminetti). He was visiting professor in London and a traveling lecturer in the United States. He has founded and manages in Varese La Piccola Fenice, a cultural center, and created the Guido Morselli Award for Unpublished Fiction. He is a contributor to the Italian television broadcast corporation RAI.

Silvio Raffo
Voice from the Stone
©2017

Made in the USA
Middletown, DE
26 April 2020

91816025R00096